A DEADLY SKIRMISH

Instantly, the three Narn vessels went to full thrusters and headed around Sheridan's Starfury toward the Centauri battle cruiser.

Space was filled with traded shots, and Sheridan helplessly listened to radio traffic.

"I think we've hit their vortex generator!" came an excited Narn voice.

"Prepare to die, Narn dogs!" a Centauri voice spat.

A Centauri shot hit one of G'Kar's flanking ships head on and it disintegrated into pieces. At the same time, the two remaining Narn fighters, ignoring Sheridan's pleas, bore down directly on the transport. As they watched, one of the Narn ships hit the battle cruiser dead center, while the other seemed to be swallowed whole by it.

"Cap—" came G'Kar's voice, before it was cut off.

"Lord, do you think . . ." Simmons blurted out.

"I don't know what happened to him. But I think we should get back to Babylon 5 before things get worse."

Leading all the Starfuries, Sheridan turned away from the recently completed battle, leaving the Centauri ship, seemingly crippled, to rake new fire upon the Worm . . .

Look for

Voices, BABYLON 5, BOOK #1
Accusations, BABYLON 5, BOOK #2
Blood Oath, BABYLON 5, BOOK #3
Clark's Law, BABYLON 5, BOOK #4

in your local bookshop

BABYLON 5:

THE TOUCH OF YOUR SHADOW, THE WHISPER OF YOUR NAME

Neal Barrett, Jr.

Based on the series by
J. Michael Straczynski

BOXTREE

First published in the UK in 1996 by Boxtree Limited,
Broadwall House, 21 Broadwall, London, SE1 9PL

First published in the USA in 1996 by Dell Publishing,
a division of Bantam Doubleday Dell Publishing Group, Inc.,
1540 Broadway, New York, New York 10036

ISBN 0 7522 0158 1

This edition published by arrangement with Dell Publishing, a division of Bantam Doubleday Dell Publishing Group Inc., New York, New York, USA

10 9 8 7 6 5 4 3 2

Printed and bound in Great Britain by
Cox & Wyman Ltd., Reading, Berkshire.

A CIP catalogue entry for this book is available from the British Library.

To Bob Vardeman,
Space Cadet

Historian's Note: The Events of this Novel take place in early 2260, before the episode "A Day in the Strife."

CHAPTER 1

There's no place like home.

Michael Garibaldi almost laughed at the thought—but, in a strange way, it was true. He *did* miss Babylon 5, and was looking forward to returning to it. The looming jump gate of Euphrates sector, which sat like a patient, hungry, metal-gridded mouth waiting to swallow both Garibaldi and the transport *Simak* he inhabited, signaled not only the end of a well-deserved vacation filled with peace and quiet, but a return to a place where both peace and quiet were at a premium. If Garibaldi thought hard about it, he could not recall twenty minutes in his stint as Babylon 5's security chief where peace had not been threatened with imminent war, and quiet had not been shattered by, well, *noise.*

And he was looking forward to going back to this?

Garibaldi, you must be nuts, he said to himself.

Ah, well, maybe things would be different when he got back.

Maybe there would be . . . peace and quiet.

"You ready to go home, Mike?" Bill Smollens, pilot of the *Simak,* asked from his seat beside Garibaldi. Smollens grinned, knowing that the upcoming jump in Smollens's crate was not exactly what Garibaldi had been looking forward to since getting up this morning.

"Having second thoughts about hitching that ride with me, Mike?" Smollens laughed.

"Not exactly," Garibaldi said grimly, trying not to look outside as the metal grid drew closer to the *Simak.* "And if you remember, 'hitching a ride' had nothing to do with it. You're merely paying off a bet, Smollens. Or have you already forgotten that little World Series wager?"

"No"—Smollens laughed—"but I'm working on it!"

Punching the transport's thrusters, the *Simak* shot ahead, into the vortex, as Michael Garibaldi groaned and tried not to look. He had forgotten what a wreck Smollens's ship was, and was now convinced that they'd never make it through in one piece.

"Is there time to turn around?" he said miserably, as Smollens's laugh became even louder.

Hyperspace opened in front of them. It looked like what it was: the warping of space, time and light, a donut hole of infinite black that was the jump point giving way to the deep crimson of hyperspace itself. They rode through these wide patches of red for several hours before the *Simak* was spit out in a blue-shifted blurt of energy back into normal space. To Garibaldi it was like being on the biggest carnival attraction in the universe—with some of the cotter pins missing from the car he was in.

"Ya-hooo!" Smollens shouted, turning to slap Garibaldi on the back as the stars returned to their normal place in the heavens and Garibaldi's stomach returned to its normal place in his body. "Epsilon sector here we are! And my old bucket of bolts made it again! That's one less debt to worry about!"

"The next time," Garibaldi said, "I'll take it out in credits."

Smollens laughed and shook his head in satisfaction, heading the *Simak* straight for Babylon 5.

And then, there it was: home.

Garibaldi felt a surge of something approaching pride. It was strange to feel this about any single place. Garibaldi had been many places before Babylon 5. He had been a shuttle pilot, head of security at a mining colony, among many other things—but he had never felt the kind of *ownership* he felt when it came to Babylon 5. Maybe it was because this was the first time that life hadn't thrown a monkey wrench into the works when things were going well. There had been plenty of problems in the past, and it always seemed that when things began to hum for Michael Garibaldi, someone, or something, decided it was time to pour molasses into the clockwork. Not that Garibaldi whined about it; but he was always on guard for the sound of that molasses container being opened.

As the *Simak* was secured with grapples and pulled into cargo bay 8, Smollens turned to Garibaldi and grinned.

"Hey, Mike, can I buy you a drink? I can't wait to get down to Brown sector. There's a little action there that I left unfinished . . ."

Garibaldi shook his head. "No, Tom, sorry. Once I get off this wreck you call a ship I've got to work. Maybe another time."

With a solid bump the *Simak* came to rest in the cargo bay, and Smollens was already unhooking himself, looking forward to his free time.

"Well, see you around then, Mike," Smollens said.

"Not if I see you first," Garibaldi said.

Smollens laughed and then was gone, leaving Garibaldi to savor a few last minutes of peace and quiet.

Perhaps, as he had thought, things really would be peaceful when he went back on duty.

But almost as if his thoughts had been read by a Psi Corps telepath, his link, silent this last week as he had lain under a warm double-sun listening to waves slap languidly against a sandy beach in Euphrates sector, sounded with a chime, and a frantic ensign's voice said, "Chief Garibaldi, please report to Brown deck at once!"

CHAPTER 2

At first Garibaldi thought that Tom Smollens had somehow managed to instantly get himself into trouble. But that was impossible; Smollens only had a few minutes' head start on Garibaldi, and in fact the security chief ran into the angry freighter pilot, who was pacing impatiently outside a guarded lift tube along with an impatient crowd.

"Mike!" Smollens said as Garibaldi approached. "They won't let anybody down to Brown deck!"

Gently disengaging himself from Smollens, Garibaldi said, "I'll see what the problem is, Tom. Why don't you check out your quarters in the meantime?"

"Sure, Mike," Smollens said, sensing that Garibaldi was now on duty and not wanting to interfere. "Maybe I'll see you later."

Nodding absently, Garibaldi had already turned his attention from the retreating pilot to the security officer guarding the lift tube entrance.

"What's the problem, Perley?"

Perley shook her head. "I don't know, chief. All I know is the Consortium of Live Eaters somehow found their way down to Brown deck, and now there's pretty much a riot down there."

"The *what?"*

"Consortium of Live Eaters," the officer repeated. Then she said, "Oh, yeah, chief, I forgot. You've been away."

"What the—" Garibaldi said, but at that moment another officer trotted up to them and said frantically, "A fight's broken out at the Trinocular Film Festival! And those Life in Transition crazies have started another ruckus in the Main Hall!"

"Damn!" officer Perley swore; to Garibaldi she said, "Chief, should I go to the Main Hall or stay here? The Life in Transition bunch is about the worst of all of them, and if they don't get help over there, there could be a lot of damage done."

Garibaldi said, "The Life in *what*?"

"Transition!" Perley looked about to burst, as did the other officer. "Chief, what should we do?"

Garibaldi, putting aside his confusion, snapped, "Perley, you stay here, and you, Rupnick, get over to that Trinocular thing. Both of you call for backup. I'll go to the Main Hall myself."

To Garibaldi's dismay, he saw relief wash over both of the officers' faces.

"Is this Life group that bad?" Garibaldi asked.

In answer, Perley gave a very emphatic nod.

"The worst," she said.

"Great," Garibaldi said, heading off for the Main Hall.

So much for peace.

And quiet.

Garibaldi had seen plenty of riots in his day—but never anything quite like this. Ever since word had spread of a mass religious experience in the garden late last year, there had been an influx of zealots of every stripe. Conflict was inevitable.

Before he even reached the Main Hall he heard the shouting.

"Go home, Lite-heads!" someone was chanting, and this was picked up by several other voices.

"GO HOME, LITE-HEADS!"

But almost as loud was another chant, many voices in a calm, steady mantra intoning, "You are mistakes. You are unnatural. You are random."

Garibaldi grabbed a civilian leaving the hall and asked, "What's going on in there?"

"They're out of their minds!" the man, a short human with a beard, which marked him as a member of the rational Combari religious sect, said. "They think none of us deserve to be here!"

"Who's 'they'?" Garibaldi said.

"Lite-heads! LITs! They think life is an aberration, a mistake, a cosmic boo-boo! They say the odds are so long against life ever springing up anywhere, anytime, that all of us are nothing but anomalies!" The man's face became red with anger. "They say there's no room for God in the universe!"

"Uh-oh," Garibaldi said, letting the man go, and now realizing just what he was up against. A religious war was just about the worst kind of mess he could have to deal with. Into his link he said, "Garibaldi to Station House. I'm in the Main Hall. I want heavy backup sent here immediately."

"On the way, Chief," came the response.

Taking a deep breath, all thoughts of his vacation and what he had hoped to find on his return to Babylon 5 banished, Garibaldi pushed his way into the Main Hall.

In the middle of the hall a low barricade had been erected from furniture. Behind this wall, the LITs had positioned themselves.

They were by far one of the oddest groups Garibaldi had ever seen. They were fully clothed, from head to foot, but not in clothing, per se. They wore what appeared to Garibaldi to be suits fashioned of slices of mineral mica linked to chunks of unprocessed ores: coal, silver, copper. What parts of their bodies could be seen were encrusted with what looked like dirt and caked mud, and their faces and bald heads were completely covered in this grainy substance.

I'd hate to have their cleaning bills, Garibaldi thought.

Surrounding the barricade were members of various religious groups, trying to hear themselves above each other, above the chants of "GO HOME, LITE-HEADS!" and above the LITs' own gravelly rumble of, "You are mistakes, you are unnatural, you are random."

As Garibaldi approached the maelstrom, he was relieved to see help arriving: a squad of his security forces was already lining the perimeter and enclosing the trouble.

Above the din, Garibaldi shouted, "All right, people! It's time for this little party to end!"

He was ignored, until he said, "Anyone still in this area in three minutes will be arrested!"

All sound save for the rhythmic mantra of the LITs ceased, and with the help of Garibaldi's people, the room was soon emptying peacefully out.

But one Narn, barely containing his fury, waved his fist in front of Garibaldi's face. "This is an outrage! These LITs should be inserted into the nearest waste receptacle! Imagine! They dare to call my people . . . *mistakes*!"

The Narn moved on, talking only to himself now, while Garibaldi wryly thought, *There have been times . . .*

With only the LIT contingent to deal with now, Garibaldi approached the barricade, which was being dismantled by two security people, leaving a gap for Garibaldi to enter.

"Which one of you people is in charge?" Garibaldi said.

The chant continued: "You are mistakes. You are unnatural. You are random."

"Hey!" Garibaldi shouted. "I expect to be heard, here! What I said a few moments ago goes for you, too! Who's in charge?"

The chant continued, but at a lower volume. A voice, from which of the LITs Garibaldi couldn't tell, said, "No one is in charge. Only the universe is in charge. As life forms, we are anomalies. We should not be here. There is nothing to celebrate."

"Would you like to celebrate a jail cell?" Garibaldi said.

The chant lowered even more.

"We did not mean to create a disturbance."

From behind Garibaldi an ensign snorted. "Right! That's the fifth disturbance they've caused in three days!"

Garibaldi quieted the security officer with a look and turned back to the LITs. "Well?"

"We merely are," the untraceable voice said. "We have no reason to be here, so we have no rights. You may do with us as you please."

Garibaldi felt like throwing his hands up.

"Where have you been meeting?" he said.

"Conference Chamber D."

"Go back there. And don't leave."

"Very well."

As a group, their chant increasing, the LITs moved off in the direction of Conference Chamber D.

"They'll be back," Stolz, the ensign who had spoken previously, said. "They stay in the conference room for a little while, then they wander out and start trouble again. It's like they have no idea what they're doing."

"Maybe they don't," Garibaldi said. "But there *is* something we can do to keep them in there. Post a doubled guard at the conference chamber door, and don't let them out. Maybe that'll take care of their disturbances. And since they don't believe they should be alive, they shouldn't protest."

The ensign nodded. "Did you have a nice leave, Chief?"

"What leave?" Garibaldi said. "It feels like I never left."

At that moment his link chimed.

"Garibaldi here."

"This is Sheridan. Please report to the briefing room immediately, Chief. We've got more trouble than we can handle."

"I'll be right there," Garibaldi said, signing off. To the ensign, he said, "Check in with Perley and Rupnick. I sent them off to handle two other disturbances. Make sure they have enough help, and if they need backup, send it to them."

"Right, Chief."

Rolling his eyes as he headed off to the briefing room, Garibaldi repeated to himself, "Like I never left . . ."

CHAPTER 3

SITTING alone in the briefing room, Captain Sheridan looked about as haggard as Garibaldi had ever seen him.

"Sorry to bring your leave to such an abrupt close, Chief," Sheridan said, gesturing Garibaldi into one of the briefing room's chairs, "but we've got our hands more than full at the moment and I don't have time for niceties. As soon as Commander Ivanova gets here we have to come up with a plan to handle this mess we're in."

"You mean all these conferees?" Garibaldi said. "That's an easy one. Just lock them all in their rooms and forget about them."

Garibaldi was a little surprised to see that his

levity did nothing to dent Sheridan's serious demeanor.

"That's not our biggest problem, Chief," the captain said.

"What—" Garibaldi began to ask, but at that moment the door slid open and in walked Commander Susan Ivanova, Executive Officer of Babylon 5.

"Commander, thanks for coming," Captain Sheridan said. "Please sit down."

Commander Ivanova, as grim-looking as Sheridan, took a seat next to Garibaldi and, after giving him a brief glance of welcome, turned her attention back to the captain.

Garibaldi, as confused as when he had walked in, turned his own attention back to the captain.

Sheridan took a deep breath and began.

"As Chief Garibaldi has already seen, we seem to be in the midst of a particularly . . . volatile period on Babylon 5. Various conferences have been scheduled at the same time, and some of these groups have come into conflict with other groups of opposing views.

"As you know, we've had more than one convention taking place on Babylon 5 in the past, and except for the Psi Corps debacle we've never had much more than minor problems. But this time, for some reason, things are worse. At first we thought this was due to the nature of some of these groups—"

Again the door opened, and in walked Dr. Stephen Franklin, Chief of Staff of Babylon 5's medical division.

"Sorry I'm late, Captain," Franklin apologized, taking an empty chair. "That surgery on that Narn's hand took longer than I anticipated."

"You came at a good time, Doctor. As I was saying," the captain continued, "we initially thought that the unusually high number of incidents was due to the nature of the groups themselves. But this has proved not to be the case. It . . . seems that many of those aboard Babylon 5 have begun to have nightmares."

"Nightmares?" Garibaldi asked.

"Terrible ones. Confusing and vivid. And there doesn't seem to be any source we can trace for them."

"Have you thought of the food?" Garibaldi laughed.

This time, to Garibaldi's relief, the slightest smile came to the captain's features.

"Yes, we've thought of the food," Dr. Franklin said. "And of the air. We've checked the oxygen generators, as well as the methane generators in the alien sector. We've scanned for viruses and bacterial agents. All the food has been checked for contaminants. In fact, that was the first place we looked. It seems there have been food contaminations in the past that were responsible for hallucinations and such. The computer found an entry for an entire French town on Earth once going essentially insane after eating bread that had been contaminated with a hallucinogen called LSD. But this is nothing like that.

"These are nightmares. Bad dreams at night, and during the day an onset of general tension, unrest, feelings of hostility and depression. Stims have been ineffective, except to keep people awake—and you can't do that forever. Not everyone on board Babylon 5 has undergone these things to the same degree, but the effect seems to be intensifying. Yet there doesn't seem to be any cause within Babylon 5 itself."

"Are you suggesting something outside the station is affecting it?" Garibaldi asked.

Commander Ivanova spoke up. "We don't know what to think."

"I can see we've got a real problem here," Garibaldi said.

Captain Sheridan nodded in agreement. "Like I said, Chief, I'm sorry your leave is over, but we've got real work to do. We've got to track down the source of these nightmares before they get worse and totally disrupt the workings of Babylon 5. Does anyone have any thoughts?"

Garibaldi answered, "As a start, I'd take seriously what I said before about locking all these conferees in their meeting chambers. If they can't get at each other, they can't start trouble, right?"

Sheridan rubbed his chin. "That's a good idea, though there may be some diplomatic hurdles to getting it accomplished. We've already had complaints from Ambassador G'Kar and Ambassador Delenn, and I would hate to see any full-blown diplomatic scenes erupt over any of this. We can at least restrict the conferees' movements as much as possible, citing security reasons. I'll leave that to you, Chief."

"Consider it done," Garibaldi said.

"The main point here," Sheridan said, "is that something is attacking Babylon 5, and we don't know what it is. Until the source of these nightmares is found, and until we understand what sort of threat it poses to us, we have to assume that whatever the source is, it is hostile. That means heightened alert for everyone, and for every department. Understood?"

There were nods of assent around the table.

"Good. Then I assume the three of you will keep me informed of anything that relates to our little meeting here today. In other words, I want to know about anything—*anything*—that might shed light on this crisis, and I want to know about it immediately, day or night."

Again, there were nods.

"This meeting is over, then," Sheridan concluded.

Captain Sheridan stayed in his chair. Garibaldi got up with the two others, but let them file out first. He stopped at the doorway and looked back at the captain.

"Sir?"

Sheridan looked up, his eyes showing strain.

"Have you been having these nightmares, too?"

Sheridan hesitated a moment before answering, "Yes, Garibaldi, I have."

CHAPTER 4

SOMETHING . . .

To Martina Coles, it came as a whisper in her mind. Not a voice; more like the edges of one—or the breaking of waves on a distant shore. There, yet not there . . .

Something . . .

Whatever it was, she had never heard anything like it before. Not in all her years in Psi Corps—from the moment she had read her little brother, quite abruptly, while they were playing in the backyard one day, to the time when Psi Corps had become aware of her abilities during a routine test, and she had been taken from her parents at the age of eight and brought under Psi Corps's all-enclosing wing. In all the years of schooling, of training, of work—she had never heard anything, any *voice,* like this.

Something . . .

Ever since she had stepped on board Babylon 5, three days before, she had felt it. At first she had thought it might be a quality of Babylon 5 itself—an ultrahigh frequency emanation from one of the station's systems. But no, this was something else.

Something . . .

Martina Coles shivered.

Deep down in Babylon 5's alien quarters, Vorlon Ambassador Kosh stood in contemplation. Around him, the fog of his own atmosphere swirled around his loosened encounter suit. It was good to be at least partially free of the cumbersome suit, with its huge shoulders and luxurious drapes of cloth, which hid Kosh's true form from the other inhabitants of Babylon 5. It was good to breathe atmosphere outside the suit.

But not everything was good.

In his alien mind, something swirled, as troublesome to Kosh as his own atmosphere would be to a human.

Something which shook Kosh to the core of his alien being . . .

Delenn, asleep and dreaming, found herself with a weapon, a curved scimitar, in her hand.

How odd.

She stared down at it for a second, as if it had landed there like a meteorite, or grown there like an unwanted fungus. For a member of the Grey Council, an ambassador, to hold a weapon in her hand was unthinkable. It was . . .

"Defend yourself, or die!"

The words were spoken so harshly, from such an unlikely source, that Delenn looked up from the weapon to see Captain John Sheridan advancing toward her, anger in his eyes, his own sword held out menacingly before him.

"Captain, I . . ."

"I said defend yourself, or die!"

Lips pulled back in hatred, Sheridan rushed forward, making a thrust with his scimitar that Delenn was forced to counter.

"Captain, please . . . !"

Again, John Sheridan tried to cut her, and again she countered the blow with her own sword, holding it firmly with both hands. She searched Sheridan's face, looking for a spark of sanity, but found none.

"Captain, why are you doing this?"

"Haven't you heard, Ambassador?" Sheridan shouted. "We're at war again! The Earth and the Minbari—and this time it's to the death!"

With a grunt, Captain Sheridan slashed at Delenn; the blow caught her own sword but drove her back.

"Captain, we must talk about this—"

"Enough talk! We've been talking for years and it's gotten us nowhere! There's only room for one of our races, and if I have anything to do with it, you and your people will be driven to extinction!"

There followed two slashing blows, the second of which drove Ambassador Delenn to the ground.

"Captain, I thought we . . ."

Sheridan loomed over her angrily. "You thought what? That we were friends? That we perhaps had feelings for one another? Didn't you hear me, Delenn—I said this is war!"

Delenn watched the powerful downward drive of his slashing scimitar, and knew she would be powerless as it drove into her body—

G'Kar, also dreaming, would be a hero!

A hero in peace, and a hero in war—that was his view of himself. He saw himself showered with gifts, paraded through all of Narn, standing tall in a stately pose, perhaps pulled on a cart drawn by two Centauri slaves: one of them, ideally, Londo Mollari.

Yes! That was the way it would be!

But first . . .

"G'Kar, we are closing on the Centauri ships," his second in command reported.

"Good," G'Kar said. "Soon they will taste the steel of Narn resolve. Lock on your targets!"

"Targets locked," came the reply.

"Fire when ready!"

G'Kar practiced his stately pose as he waited for the welcoming hiss of the guns firing through empty space, driving into the advancing Centauri ships—

Nothing happened.

"I said fire your weapons!" G'Kar shouted, still trying to retain his dignified pose.

Again, nothing happened.

His second in command reported, "Our weapons are frozen! The Centauri are flooding us with some new kind of scan that's preventing us from firing!"

G'Kar lost his pose as he bent desperately over the console. "Override it, you fool!"

"I . . . can't!"

At that moment there came a roar which rocked the ship, as the advancing Centauri fleet peppered his ship with debilitating fire.

"We have a message from the Centauri!"

Without G'Kar's permission, the face of Londo Mollari filled the screen.

"Ha! G'Kar!"

"This is an outrage! We will annihilate you!" G'Kar raged.

"I don't think so, G'Kar," Londo said. The fan of his hair seemed to have grown, making him appear even more like a strutting Earth peacock. "In fact, I have special plans for you."

"We're disabled!" G'Kar's second in command shouted. "We're helpless!"

On the screen, Londo Mollari began to laugh, as he held up a collar and leash.

"This," Londo responded laughing, "is reserved especially for you, G'Kar!"

Garibaldi, asleep too, opened his mouth to speak, but nothing came out.

He found himself in the pilot's seat of a shuttle, staring out at an unfamiliar patch of space.

He was about to ask himself, "Where am I?" when he knew.

Sound filtered into his ears, and he found he could speak now. He heard a voice behind him, and turned to see Susan Ivanova.

She put her hand on his shoulder. "Are we there yet?"

"I . . . think so," Garibaldi said.

Ivanova laughed and said, "What, no wisecracks? You're not worried, are you?"

"Of course not," Garibaldi snapped. Forcing a laugh, he added, "What, me worry?"

Before him, suddenly, a planet appeared, swirling sickly orange, looming large. Already, they were within its gravitational pull, and Garibaldi felt the shuttle edging ineluctably into the thick atmosphere.

"Taking it a little steep, aren't you?" Ivanova queried, a tinge of worry climbing into her voice.

"I . . . don't seem to have a choice," Garibaldi said, suddenly aware that he had next to no control over the shuttle.

The shuttle nosed down and drove into the tops of the orange clouds.

"Um . . . is this place maybe made of rubber?" Garibaldi uttered, helplessly fighting with the unresponsive controls.

"Michael, do you know what you're doing?" Ivanova exclaimed, reaching over to take the controls away from him.

"Of course I do!" he shouted back, but suddenly

he was sweating, not knowing if he was in control or not, *not trusting himself* . . .

The clouds drew away above them, and now a butter-colored landscape spread out below them, dotted with brownish clumps of vegetation.

"Let me do it!" Ivanova demanded, trying to tear the controls out of Garibaldi's hands. But he made a split-second decision and pushed her away.

"I can do it, dammit!"

Hands firmly on the controls, he watched the yellow landscape drive up at them, a sand-filled valley spreading like a table below them, flattening out, inviting Garibaldi to pull up and land gently.

The controls freed in his hands, he began to pull the nose up—

"We're gonna make it!" he shouted.

Then there was a flash from below—then another—and Garibaldi caught sight of battle emplacements as the shuttle suddenly pitched forward, its nose down again straight into the compacted sand—

"Nooooo!"

Covered in cold sweat, Michael Garibaldi sat up in bed. His breath came in hard gasps.

It was only after a few moments that he was able to orient himself, and to realize that his link was sounding.

Unable to catch his breath, he wiped sweat from his brow before answering the chirp.

"Garibaldi here."

There was a pause from the other end, and then

Susan Ivanova's voice said, "Garibaldi, are you all right?"

A shiver at hearing Ivanova's voice went through Garibaldi, but he managed to get out, "Sure. Good as can be."

"Well, I hope so, because we've got more trouble on our hands. Some of it's at Security Central. And there's a meeting in the briefing room in fifteen minutes."

"I'll be . . . there."

"Right."

The link went dead, and Garibaldi stared at it for a moment.

Any trouble is better than what I just went through, he thought.

CHAPTER 5

GARIBALDI felt as if he were walking through the land of the unliving.

No one on Babylon 5 seemed to be asleep. Every hallway was jammed with the awakened—and the haunted-looking. Garibaldi passed two minor skirmishes and two others about to break out. In the air there was the unmistakable smell of tension—and Garibaldi knew that where there was tension there was the chance for big trouble.

Garibaldi hurried into Security Central, expecting to find a haven of professionalism and calm. Instead what he found was a shouting match in full bloom, as two of his officers, Martin and Kristian, battled over manning a single instrumentation screen. Garibaldi thought the argument would end automatically at his appearance—but instead it intensified.

"All right—that's enough!" Garibaldi ordered, and the two men stopped their argument, looked at Garibaldi, then, incredibly, resumed their fight!

"I was here for my shift on time!"

"And I told you—I'm working overtime to send extra credits home!"

"And I—"

Striding forward, Garibaldi grabbed a fistful of each officer's uniform and drove them face-to-face into one another. He brought his own face close to theirs and said, "Now hear this! You have two choices: to end this nonsense or end up in the brig! Clear?"

The two officers mumbled, "Yes, Chief."

"Good!"

Garibaldi let them go, walked away, and immediately heard them go at it again.

"That's it!" Garibaldi shouted. He called to two other officers, watching from the far corner of the room. "Take those two to the brig!" he ordered.

The other two nodded in obedience and escorted the two offenders out of Security Central.

To the remaining officer in the room, Garibaldi asked, "What's going on, Coyle?"

"Just another riot, Chief. The Fermi's Angels are still burned over the Life in Transition group being on Babylon 5, so they ran their Plasma Hogs through the Brown deck. Wrecked a couple of vendor carts, and—"

Garibaldi had held up his hand a few words into

this report. "Fermi's Angels? The fundamentalist physicist bunch?"

"That's them. You should see the motorcycles they've built. Exact replicas of ancient Harley-Davidsons. A beautiful thing to behold—until they started running amok with them, of course—"

"Of course," Garibaldi repeated. He scanned the screens, looking for more trouble, and had no trouble finding any: it seemed in every corner of Babylon 5 there was either a fistfight or a riot in the making.

"How many people are on duty now?"

"Regular shifts." The officer grinned. "Except for Martin and Kristian, who were fighting until you threw them in the brig."

Garibaldi said, "I want doubled patrols, from this moment until further notice."

"Yes, Chief."

"If you want me, I'll be with Captain Sheridan." Garibaldi gave the officer a level stare. "And don't hesitate to call me."

"Yes, Chief."

"Fermi's Angels . . ." Garibaldi said under his breath, shaking his head as he headed for the briefing room.

Captain Sheridan, who looked as tired as Garibaldi felt, said, "Dr. Franklin can't be here now, because there are too many injured to attend to from tonight's unrest. However, he is starting a study, at my orders, on the nightmare plague that seems to be affecting Babylon 5. Also, I have informed Earth Central of our plight, and they tell me they have people down there studying the problem. I assume I am not the only one who has had bad dreams tonight?"

Susan Ivanova, looking worn-out, said, "Oh, yes—a doozy," and Garibaldi nodded his assent also.

Sheridan said, "I have called a discreet meeting to be held twenty-four hours from now, which will include the Minbari and Centauri ambassadors, as well as G'Kar. I invited Kosh, also, but he declines to attend. I get the feeling . . . whatever this thing is, Kosh is bothered by it as much as the rest of us."

"Why do you say that?" Garibaldi asked.

Sheridan shook his head. "Just in the way . . . he responded to my request. I must admit that for a while I entertained the thought that Ambassador Kosh might be behind all this. While I don't believe the Vorlons would do us any harm, it is possible that they would subject us to some sort of . . . experiment. Anyway, this appears not to be the case, and I'd appreciate it if you would leave my speculations in this room.

"I've also invited to our meeting someone none of you have met, a telepath named Martina Coles. She's passing through Babylon 5 on her way to assignment elsewhere, but she's the only telepath we have at the moment and I want her input."

Garibaldi broke in. "Is that totally wise, Captain?"

Sheridan replied, "How do you mean?"

Garibaldi looked at Ivanova before answering.

"Well, you know the way Psi Corps is, Captain. I mean, I wouldn't be surprised if they were capable of cooking up something like this nightmare plague themselves. We had trouble enough with Talia . . ."

"I'm quite aware of what you're saying, Chief, and you aren't bringing up anything I haven't already considered myself. But from what Dr. Franklin and the scientific staff tell me, this phenomenon is not emanating from within Babylon 5. Therefore, I think we can rule Martina Coles out as some sort of Psi Corps spy, at least in this matter. She may be able to give us some additional information."

"I don't think we have anything to lose," Ivanova said, surprising Garibaldi. "And since the disturbance seems to be mental, it's her area of expertise."

"As bad as the prevalent nightmares are to the inhabitants and staff of Babylon 5," Sheridan went on, "much more troubling to me is the fact that these nightmares seem to be leading to more dangerous behavior. Besides the effects of a general lack of sleep, everyone on Babylon 5 seems to be growing tense and short-tempered."

Garibaldi leaned forward onto the table. "There are fights breaking out constantly all over the station. I just had to break up a fight between two of my own men."

Sheridan nodded. "I have a feeling that things are going to get a lot worse on Babylon 5 before they get better. I want all of us to be aware of it, and be ready. The whole place is on edge, almost as if everyone were waiting for something—"

The captain's link sounded, and he said, "Sheridan here."

"Captain? This is the Observation Dome. I . . . think you should come up here, sir."

"What is it? Trouble?"

"Not exactly, sir. That is, I'm not sure."

Impatient and tired, Sheridan snapped, "Would you please speak plainly?"

"I really don't know what to say, Captain. Except that you should come and see this for yourself."

"See what?"

"This thing, Captain. Outside Babylon 5. This thing that's just appeared out of nowhere."

CHAPTER 6

It was a broad band of green, like a tightly woven veil of small, intensely bright stars. Its shape was irregular, like a long and ragged ribbon against the darkness of space.

"It looks like a worm," Garibaldi said.

Captain Sheridan, standing beside the security chief and viewing the thing through the Observation Dome's curved windows, agreed. "Yes it does. But what is it?"

Commander Ivanova, her own curiosity as to the anomaly's physical appearance sated, now manned the large curved control console. Her eyes darted over data screens, and a frown formed on her features.

"It . . . doesn't seem to be anything at all."

Frowning himself, Sheridan turned from the wondrous sight and asked, "Will you explain that, Commander?"

"I mean that, according to our instruments, that green worm out there is at the moment twenty light years away from Babylon 5. It's"—Ivanova consulted a screen—"nine million miles long, and, at its widest point, it's a half million miles wide. But, though we can measure its dimensions, according to what I'm being told here, it's an illusion. It doesn't physically exist." Her eyes moved from Sheridan to the curved windows. "It's just not there."

"That's impossible!" Sheridan said impatiently. "It *has* to be there if we can see it and measure it!"

"It seems to take up dimension, but no space," Ivanova said. "At least, that's what this data is telling me."

Sheridan's impatience overflowed. "I can't accept that," he said. "There are other tests that can be made. I want a science team on it right away."

"Yes, Captain," Ivanova said.

Sheridan turned to Garibaldi, who continued to study the green worm with interest. "Mr. Garibaldi, I want a general bulletin posted throughout Babylon 5 that we've encountered something new and are seeking to investigate it. Put it in nonthreatening words, something to the effect of, 'A wonderful opportunity for research.' I don't want anyone on Babylon 5 getting any strange ideas—at least not until they're warranted."

Without turning from his study of the Worm, Garibaldi said, "We can send that bulletin out, but I doubt it will keep some of the groups we have on board at the moment from getting funny ideas."

"Do the best you can, Chief."

"Of course."

"And I don't have to tell either of you that our little upcoming meeting is even more important now. We have to get on top of this situation before it gets on top of us." He glanced with displeasure at the beautiful band of green shimmering far outside the window. "This is just what we need, on top of all this business with the nightmares."

Garibaldi turned away from the window. "Have you considered that perhaps they're related? It does seem a little too much of a coincidence that the Worm shows up at the same time all of us are having bad dreams."

"If the Worm even exists . . ." Ivanova said.

Sheridan looked from one to the other. "Yes, well, regardless of what the truth is, I'd say all of us have our hands full at the moment. I will see both of you at that meeting, but in the meantime, we all have duties to attend to. Garibaldi, I'd like you to get to work on that bulletin immediately, and Ivanova, I'd appreciate it if you'd stay here at Command and Control and monitor the Worm. I'm going to talk to Earth Central. They need to be informed about this new development."

As he left, Garibaldi and Ivanova turned back to the window.

"What next?" Ivanova wondered aloud.

* * *

In his office, Captain Sheridan tried to banish the tiredness from his face by sprucing up and combing his hair before facing the communication screen and opening a Gold Channel to Earth Central. He knew he had only been partly successful by the look on the official's face that greeted him.

"Having trouble, Captain?" Hilton Dowd, aide to President Clark, asked.

"Actually, yes. I thought President Clark should be made aware of the fact that we seem to have—"

"We know what you've encountered."

"How—?" the captain began to ask, but the official held up his hand.

"A . . . freighter about to enter the Epsilon Sector jump gate reported the appearance of the green band to Earthforce. The president is . . . very interested in knowing what it is."

"That's just the problem. We don't know what it is. We've been able to measure its length and width, but our scanners tell us that it doesn't physically exist."

For the first time in their conversation, the man on the screen looked ruffled. "How far away is it from Babylon 5 at the moment?"

"Twenty light years."

"That seems a safe enough distance. But we would like you to use every means at your disposal to find out what it is. And what kind of threat it poses."

Sheridan started to say, "We're not sure it poses any thr—" when the other cut him off again.

"Get some sleep if you can, Captain. And keep us posted."

The Gold Channel was cut off and the screen went dark, leaving John Sheridan alone.

What kind of threat . . .

CHAPTER 7

AGAIN, something touched Martina Coles's mind. Two things, actually.

One was that strange, unknowable thing she had felt earlier in the night, the insubstantial brush of invisible fingers across her brain. The other, the second touching, was of something she knew, or at least vaguely understood. It was a being on Babylon 5, of that she was sure, but one she had never had any contact with before.

Alien.

The thought shook her to the very core of her being. She let out an audible gasp, getting up from her bed to stand with her back against the nearest wall. Fear gripped her like a cold iron hand. She felt herself frozen with terror, sweat breaking out on her body.

Suddenly she was physically ill, and it was all she could do to stumble to the bathroom before she retched over the toilet, shaking with cold fear.

Alien.

The thought of an alien touching her mind, somehow reaching out to her . . .

Again her stomach turned over, and now she was on her knees, gripping the toilet to keep from fainting.

Vorlon—

The alien reaching out to her mind suddenly retreated, and with a deep breath Martina became herself again.

Continuing to take deep breaths, she stood up slowly and poured herself a glass of water with trembling fingers.

She drank, the memory of what had just occurred to her sending a final shiver through her slight body.

With a final deep breath she straightened and surveyed the mess that the bathroom had become.

Giving a shiver not of fear now but of disgust, she cleaned the toilet, disrobed and vibe-showered, and dressed in a severe black suit and black boots. Except for her head, her body was completely covered. Her black hair was cut severely short; on her pale face she wore no makeup. Her short nails sported no polish.

Driving all thoughts from her mind, she left her room, found the nearest transport tube and took it down to the alien sector. Donning an environment helmet, she adjusted the oxygen and went immediately to a particular door, requesting entry.

With a hiss the door opened, letting out a fog of methane from which her helmet sheltered her.

Martina entered, and the door hissed closed behind her, clouding her in methane.

She took two steps and the fog swirled away, revealing the imposing figure of Kosh, hidden in his own mysterious environment suit.

Without preamble, Martina said, tight-lipped, "You reached out to my mind."

The irised cavity within Kosh's environment suit opened and closed, letting out a tinkling musical sound but no words.

Driving down the fear that sought to grip her, Martina said, "I want you to leave me alone."

Again the cavity in Kosh's suit irised open, and this time human speech was heard. "You are . . . not ready to hear me."

"You're damned right I'm not ready, and never will be. There's nothing I want from you. Don't touch my mind again."

The iris opened and closed. "When . . . you are ready."

"I told you never!"

Fearful of losing her control, a violent trembling at even being in the presence of an alien beginning to grip her, Martina turned and ran for the door, pounding on it when it wouldn't open fast enough and throwing herself through when it finally did open.

Outside in the hallway, she ripped the environment helmet from her head and breathed deeply, one hand on the wall steadying her. She bent over, feeling again as if her stomach were about to turn over.

"Are you all right?"

Gasping for breath, Martina looked up into the alien face of a Drazi, which tilted questioningly at her.

Shouting in surprise, Martina threw the environment helmet at the Drazi and pushed herself away, running down the hall.

It was only when she had reached her own level in the lift tube and the doors opened to the hallway outside her room, that her breath steadied, and she was able to walk without fear of fainting.

Once back in her room, she again disrobed, showered, and changed into another suit as severely black as the one she had previously worn.

Refusing to remember what had just happened to her, she sat in a straight-backed chair in her temporary quarters on Babylon 5 and emptied her mind of all thoughts, waiting for the summons from Captain Sheridan for the meeting he had asked her to attend.

An hour later, a single brief memory of her encounter reached through to her, and a single cold chill ran through her, making her shiver, before her eyes refixed on the far wall and she continued to wait.

CHAPTER 8

SLEEP was the last thing on Garibaldi's mind. After seeing to the composition of the security bulletin that would be broadcast throughout Babylon 5 regarding the appearance of the Worm, the chief had hoped to return to the Observation Dome and have another look at the green ribbon. Instead, he found himself in the middle of a combination motorcycle rally and religious demonstration.

On his way to the Observation Dome, his link called him down to Brown level, where once again Fermi's Angels were at it.

On leaving the transport tube, he was immediately confronted by the large, wide, leather jacket–covered back of a Fermi's Angel. The man's long hair, split into two braids, framed a colorful picture etched into the black leather of a split atom topped with a halo.

Someone bumped into Garibaldi from behind, pushing him into the jacketed giant, who turned around.

His wide, bearded face set into a scowl.

"You got a problem, man?"

Garibaldi sought to show the man his badge, but he was already being lifted, his jacket gripped by the biker's two fists, which resembled two whole hams.

The biker brought the security chief's face close to his own.

"I said, you got a problem?"

Garibaldi grinned sheepishly, spying what looked to be a vintage Harley-Davidson motorcycle behind the biker's giant torso. "Just . . . admiring your hog, is all."

The man's face split into a huge smile. "You like it, man?" He set the security chief down gently next to the machine. "Ain't it the finest?"

"It sure is," Garibaldi said, with genuine admiration. The security chief had seen machines resembling this one in museums, but never up close. "How many, uh, cc's is the engine?"

"Fifteen hundred, man! With a plasma-generated four stroke! Hardly any maintenance! We tried a nuke in her, but it was just too unstable . . ." The man's face brightened. "Hey, man, you want to take a ride?"

"Who—me?" Garibaldi said.

"Sure!" And suddenly the security chief was being lifted again, this time set on the seat of the Harley behind the Angel, who now kicked the hog into life.

"Name's Carbon, man!" the biker announced, reaching a hand around perilously to shake Garibaldi's own.

"Um, I'm Mike," the security chief said, shaking the hand quickly so that Carbon could return both hands to the bike's handlebars, where they belonged.

"Here we go!" Carbon shouted, and with a roar the Harley shot forward, parting the crowd.

Garibaldi was soon whooping as loudly as Carbon as they negotiated what appeared to be a homemade course through the commercial district of Brown deck. Merchants had long since pulled their portable stalls back to the very edges, leaving a fairly wide swath of clear roadway.

"Yahooooo!" Carbon shouted, taking a tight turn and nearly spinning out. "It's like heaven on earth, ain't it, Mike?"

Suddenly, Carbon's cycle was flanked by two others that roared out of alleys to either side; and, when Garibaldi glanced behind, he saw three others arranged behind them. Two of the cyclists wore helmets with a halo circling the top, and one other had a halo tattooed on his bald skull.

The biker with the halo tattoo gave Garibaldi a toothless grin and a thumbs-up.

"Yaaaaaa-hoooooooo!" Carbon called out, flooring the accelerator and shooting ahead as patrons and peddlers cowered in fear, pressing themselves as tightly as possible back away from the straightaway that the bikers had formed with their show of solidarity.

Garibaldi's heart went into his mouth as Carbon's cycle suddenly lifted its front wheel, as the biker did a wheelie.

"Hoooooo-haaaaaa!"

Around them, the other bikers answered, "Hoooooo-eeeeeee!"

Suddenly braking, Carbon brought his hog to a screeching halt, the others stopping around him, forming a circle.

"That was great, man!" the cyclist with the tattooed head exclaimed.

"The best!" another, even larger than Carbon, said, removing his helmet to reveal that he was a she.

Amid the general clamor, Garibaldi removed himself from the back of Carbon's Harley.

"What'd you think, man?" Carbon said, slapping Garibaldi on the back and grinning.

"Hey, let's make him an honorary Angel!" the woman biker said. She removed her leather jacket and threw it at Garibaldi, hitting him in the chest with it. "Try it on!"

"Yeah, try on Silicon's jacket, man!" Carbon said.

"Well," Garibaldi said, tentatively; but seeing the instant change from friendliness to suspicion that his attitude brought on, he gamely put the leather jacket on.

"I kind of like the feel of this," he said, smiling.

"So, what'd you think of the ride?" Carbon said.

"Great, just great."

"And what do you think about joining up?" Silicon said, showing off her own partial lack of teeth by smiling.

Almost regretfully, Garibaldi showed them his badge. "I think . . . you guys are going to have to take it easy with the bike rallies."

"Oh, man, he's a cop!" Silicon said ruefully.

Temporary anger was replaced by respect on Carbon's face. "Hey, he's okay, man. He's the dude that locked the Lite-heads in their conference room." He punched Garibaldi heartily on the shoulder. "Yeah, he's okay."

"Yeah, those Lite-heads got no respect for life!" Silicon said. "They got no respect for God!"

Instantly, all the bikers bowed their heads and began to mumble. Carbon, his eyes closed, said, "And Lord, who art Lord of all bikers everywhere, know that we do honor you when we ride. As ye made all men, so too did you make all physics; as ye made bikers, so too did ye make possible their bikes. For this we thank you, and honor you, and defend you all through the day, every day."

"Amen," came the chorus from Silicon and the rest. They all looked at Garibaldi expectantly.

"Amen?" Garibaldi said.

Once again, Carbon slapped him on the back. "You're great, man! And now I'm sure that you understand why we have such a basic problem with the Lite-heads."

"Umm . . . not really," Garibaldi said.

"Don't you see? They think everything came

from nothing, man! That all this beautiful physics we see around us means *nothing*! That's blasphemy! All us Fermi's Angels, we're physicists, but we see the spirituality in every particle and subparticle, in every quark and tachyon! It's all God's dance, man! Don't you see that?"

Garibaldi said, diplomatically, "I think you have every right to your beliefs, but I also think that every one of the other hundred religions on Babylon 5 has a right to their own beliefs, too—"

Real anger sparked in Carbon's face—and for the first time, Garibaldi sensed that the biker and his compatriots had been just as subject to the nightmares and sleeplessness as the rest of Babylon 5's residents.

"But they're *not* a religion, man! They're a *non*religion! A blasphemy! And they've even been giving us bad dreams, man!"

Trying to keep things under control, Garibaldi said, "Well, you're not the only ones with sleep problems, lately. All I can do is ask you to keep cool." He smiled, and patted the seat of Carbon's hog. "For the sake of the bikes, okay?"

Carbon's mood lightened. "Sure, man."

"And we'll see if we can arrange some sort of riding track for you guys, away from all these people. Maybe on one of the less populated decks."

"All right, man!"

"Good, then, in the meantime . . ." Garibaldi started to remove Silicon's leather jacket, but Carbon stopped him.

"Hey, man—that's yours now! You're an honorary member of the Angels!"

Not wanting any more provocation, and seeing the beginnings of hurt on Silicon's face, Garibaldi kept the jacket on and said, "Oh, uh, sure. Cool."

"Way cool!" Silicon said happily, giving Garibaldi a friendly punch on the arm, which hurt even more than Carbon's had.

"Yeah," Garibaldi answered, his smile more of a grimace.

CHAPTER 9

THE briefing room filled up quickly. Commander Ivanova was smart enough to place herself at the doorway, to make sure that G'Kar, the Narn representative, and Londo, the Centauri ambassador, sat as far apart as possible. This did not, of course, solve the problem of the two being in the same room.

As Londo entered, G'Kar stood and proclaimed, "I will *not* be in the same area as that . . . murderer!"

"Nor will I," said Londo, "breathe air that has been polluted by that sublife-form's inferior lungs!"

Closer to the exit, Londo sought to stalk from the room but was prevented from leaving by Commander Ivanova's presence; in a moment, G'Kar, seeking exit also, had nearly collided with Londo and the two began a debate, face-to-face:

"G'Kar, you do not represent a significant power. You have no place here."

"That is because you slaughtered my people." G'Kar raised a fist. "I don't know why I've let you continue to strut around here."

"Allowed me?" Londo put his hand on the hilt of his sword. "I could crush you like a worm. Survival of the fittest, my friend."

G'Kar yelled, "I am not your friend! No one is."

Londo straightened, and then he smiled, his eyes two chunks of black ice. "You're wrong, G'Kar. I do have friends. And they know you quite well."

Captain Sheridan's commanding voice brought all hostilities to a halt.

"I want everyone to *stop* this foolishness immediately! We're here for more important things than schoolyard sniping! G'Kar is here because we're having continuing violence between the Narn and the Centauri and it has to stop." He indicated the two empty chairs at opposite ends of the table. "Gentlemen, if you will please sit down!"

Eyeing one another venemously, the two representatives sat.

All chairs were filled save one; and Ivanova, counting heads—there was Dr. Franklin, and the Minbari Ambassador Delenn, and Garibaldi as well as Captain Sheridan—was trying to figure out who was missing when she felt a presence behind her in the open doorway.

She turned to confront the petite, black-clad figure of a stone-faced Martina Coles.

Startled, Ivanova recovered and began to introduce herself—but the telepath strode past her, tight-lipped, as if she weren't there, and took the empty place.

Under her breath, Ivanova said, "Hello to you, too," and took her own place beside Captain Sheridan.

Sheridan stood up. "I want to thank all of you for coming here. I'm sure by now you know why we needed to talk. Originally, this meeting was to discuss the recent rash of nightmares that seem to be plaguing Babylon 5. However, in the last twenty-four hours, it seems we have another problem to contend with, which may or may not be related to the nightmares—"

"The nightmares are a Centauri trick!" G'Kar shouted, unable to control himself. He rose, pointing to Londo. "They seek to destroy all surviving Narn, and along with us all friends of the Narn aboard Babylon 5!"

Londo sneered. "That is just the kind of thing a Narn would say—especially one who was responsible himself for the nightmares!" Londo too rose, pointing his own finger at G'Kar. "There, Captain, is your traitor!"

"Enough!" Captain Sheridan turned to Garibaldi, who sat with his arms crossed, patiently watching the proceedings. "Chief, if these two go at it again, I want them confined to their quarters for the foreseeable future. Is that clear?"

"It would be my pleasure, Captain," Chief Garibaldi said, giving the two startled ambassadors a mild look.

"That would be unprecedented!" G'Kar fumed.

"An outrage!" Londo concurred. "And illegal—a trampling of ambassadorial privilege!"

"Well, at least the two of you agree on one thing—that you don't want me to lock you up." Sheridan's face grew stern. "But I will do that, ambassadorial privilege or not, to preserve peace on Babylon 5! We are nearing an emergency situation. And if I see fit to declare a state of emergency, I will have that power. Do I make myself clear?"

"Yes, Captain," G'Kar said between clenched teeth, sitting down.

Londo raised a hand. "I cooperate for the sake of a solution," he said in a flat voice and sat.

"Good. And I want you two to remember that Babylon 5 is a place for diplomacy, not war. Whatever problems your two races have, they will not be acted out on Babylon 5. I'm sure if the two of you had not been subject to the recent spate of bad dreams, you would see that more clearly. I need your help and I expect to get it."

The captain straightened, giving his attention to the entire room. "As I was saying, within the last day we have been given a new phenomenon to study, which may or may not be related to our other problem. The green band of light, aptly nicknamed the Worm by Mr. Garibaldi, which all of you have no doubt witnessed for yourselves by now, has presented us with a few . . . difficulties. I've asked

Commander Ivanova, who I've put in charge of the science team studying the Worm, to summarize what they've been able to learn thus far . . . Commander?"

Sheridan sat, giving Ivanova the floor. She stood and said, "Well, I'm afraid there isn't much to report. Every scan we've run on the Worm has come up . . . empty. We've been able to measure its length, and width, and how far away from us it is. But as for anything else—well, we just get no readings at all—"

"But that is impossible!" Londo exclaimed. "How can something be so wide, and so long, and so far away, and yet not be composed of anything?"

Ivanova shrugged. "That's what we're getting, at least so far. There are other tests that the techs are devising, but they'll take a little time. And, frankly, I'm told not to expect anything."

G'Kar said thoughtfully, "Could it be that this thing is hiding behind some sort of detection barrier . . . ?"

"We thought of that," Ivanova said. "But if it was, we would be able to read that fact in our scans. In other words, you can scan *something,* and you can also scan where something *should* be. But in this case there is . . . nothing. This thing is simply not there."

"But you can *see* it," Londo said, furrowing his brow. "I have seen it myself. It is green!"

"And yet we detect no shift in its color spectrum," Ivanova said.

"Totally unprecedented," Londo replied. "Perhaps it is a new type of weapon."

"We don't know what it is," Captain Sheridan interjected, standing as Commander Ivanova sat. "And I want to emphasize that whatever speculations any of us may have, they are only that—speculations. I am counting on everyone within this room to keep what you've heard here to yourselves."

"But we have heard *nothing*!" Londo complained. He laughed derisively. "Your detectors have detected nothing!"

Trying not to grow angry at the implications in the ambassador's words, Captain Sheridan said, "That's correct." He turned to Dr. Franklin. "Have your people been able to find anything further out about the nightmare plague?"

"Plague is a good term for it—though we haven't been able to find any bug to blame it on. I had every cargo bay scanned, thinking that perhaps a virus had found its way onto Babylon 5, but nothing was found. And I'm sorry to report that there has now been one death attributable to this 'plague,' a bartender from Down Below who went crazy with lack of sleep and cut his own throat with a broken bottle."

Sheridan said to Garibaldi, "You're sure this was a suicide, Chief?"

Garibaldi nodded. "He went nuts. I know one of the witnesses, an informant who always hangs out at the Happy Daze bar; this guy said this bartender was afraid to go to sleep, kept talking about his bad dreams and how 'they' were going to get him if he dozed off again. Finally he just snapped."

Sheridan turned his attention back to Dr. Franklin. "Anything show up when he got to you?"

"Nothing unusual," Franklin reported. "I was hoping perhaps to find some anomaly in the brain tissue or elsewhere, but everything was within parameters. It was a dead end."

"So we have nothing medical and nothing physical to help us out," Sheridan said. "What about psychological?"

Franklin said, "There's a psychiatrist, Dr. Jenkins, on station who has an interesting theory. He thinks all of these nightmares are based on feelings of fear of . . . the unknown. Of suspicion of others that are not like we are. These feelings are always with us, of course; they are part of our self-defense mechanisms. But these bad dreams seem to be intensifying them."

"That's very interesting," Sheridan said. "There's another area I'd like to explore in connection with that." He nodded toward Martina Coles. "That's why I've asked Ms. Coles to join us. In fact, we've picked up a temporary contract with Psi Corps for Ms. Coles's services. Even though she's only on Babylon 5 temporarily, on her way to another job, she's the only telepath we have. She has read two consenting crew members who have been particularly bothered by nightmares before this meeting; perhaps she'll share her findings with us now?"

Captain Sheridan gave Martina a warm smile of welcome, which was not returned.

Martina said cooly, "I found only that they were bothered by deep-rooted anxieties that would normally be buried deep in their minds, but which have now been pushed to the fore."

Franklin said, "That's similar to what Dr. Jenkins said."

Martina said, unsmiling, "Is there anything else you need me for at the moment?"

Captain Sheridan said, "I thought, perhaps, you could continue your readings—"

"I will not read aliens," Martina said, flatly.

Slightly embarassed, Captain Sheridan said, "Pardon me?"

"If you study the special provisions of my contract with you, it states that I will not read aliens."

"I'm aware of that, but under the circumstances—"

Martina stood abruptly. "If you require my services, I will be in my quarters. Otherwise, I ask not to be disturbed."

Before anyone could object, she had turned and walked from the room, leaving the door sliding closed behind her.

"Well, *that's* a piece of work," Garibaldi cracked.

"And she dresses like a Psi Cop," Ivanova said.

"Captain," Londo complained, "I protest the manner in which that . . . *mind reader* referred to us representatives."

"Her use of that word simply shows the vast distance that still remains between our races," G'Kar said.

Delenn merely closed her eyes in contemplation.

Captain Sheridan said, "I do apologize to everyone for Ms. Coles. I promise to have a chat with her. In the meantime, is there anything else that needs to be discussed before we adjourn this meeting?"

Garibaldi said, "Only that security has been beefed up on all levels, but that there are still problems all over the place. I would especially like to ask the Narn and Centauri ambassadors to try to keep their people apart as much as possible. With feelings between them so rotten to begin with, this edginess over the nightmares has just made things ten times worse."

Sheridan turned to Londo and G'Kar. "Gentlemen?"

G'Kar touched his chest. "I, for my part, will certainly do what can be done."

"Spoken like a weakling," Londo said.

G'Kar stood, knocking his chair backward. "One day we will destroy you."

Londo leaned back and stretched, resting his head in his hands. "And that day is not today."

"Gentlemen!" Captain Sheridan shouted. "Remember what I said, about locking you in your quarters!"

Garibaldi smiled, and said, "Boo!"

Londo and G'Kar held their tongues.

"If no one else has anything to say, we'll end this meeting now. I count on your continued cooperation, and if the situation warrants it, we'll all meet again."

The meeting adjourned, leaving Captain Sheridan in his seat as the participants filed out, Londo and G'Kar well separated.

After the others had gone, Sheridan looked up to see that Delenn had stayed behind.

"Are you all right, Delenn?" Sheridan asked, seeing the pensive look on her face. "You didn't say anything during the meeting."

"What I had to say was for you alone to hear, Captain," she said.

"Of course," Sheridan answered.

After a moment, Delenn spoke, haltingly. "I . . . only wanted to warn you that Babylon 5 may . . . be in for more trouble than any of us can handle."

Sheridan frowned. "How do you mean? Do you know something the rest of us don't?"

"Not . . . exactly. It is only a feeling. But a very powerful one. Based on my own . . . bad dreams."

"Yes?" Sheridan said, waiting for her to elaborate.

"These . . . feelings of fear of others. They may become a grave danger to Babylon 5 and everyone on it."

"Are you implying that all of the various groups on Babylon 5 are going to turn on one another?"

"Something like that, yes."

Sheridan almost laughed, but not with humor. "But Babylon 5 is made up of nothing *but* differences! We have a quarter of a million people on this station, thousands of groups, hundreds of races, a hundred religions alone!"

Delenn looked at him with feeling. "And if all of those diversities were to turn on one another . . ."

"There would be chaos! It would tear the station apart and destroy everything we've worked for!"

"That is what I am afraid of, Captain."

Sheridan stared off at the far wall for a moment, contemplating; then abruptly he shook his head. "I can't consider that, Delenn. It's too much to even imagine. The evidence on hand doesn't yet warrant a theory that extreme. Even if it were true I don't know what action I could take."

"I, too, don't know what action you could take to avert such chaos, Captain," Delenn said quietly, "but I believe it's true and I'm afraid it will come."

"Based on what evidence?"

The sadness on Delenn's features stabbed at Captain Sheridan's heart. "Based on my own evidence, Captain. Based on my own dreams."

"And what do you dream?"

"In my dreams, these fears of otherness, of aggression and suspicion of what is alien and different, is manifested in a very unique and clear way. One that I cannot ignore."

"I still don't see," Sheridan said, wanting more than anything to remove the deep wellspring of sadness from Delenn's features.

"You see, Captain," Delenn said, "these feelings are manifested in my dreams by you. You try to kill me."

CHAPTER 10

In the Observation Dome, Commander Ivanova could barely believe her eyes.

"Are you sure?" she said to the tech manning the screen beside her; the tech's eyes were wide with the same look as Ivanova's, even though the tech was looking at numbers and not the Worm.

"Yes, Commander. It's moved. Big-time."

"I can see that," Ivanova said, as the huge twisting length of the Worm filled the curved window in front of her, where before it had been a distant sight.

"And you say it's how far away now?"

The tech said, "At its present velocity, it will reach Babylon 5 within"—the tech looked up from the screen and Ivanova could not mistake the look of fear in his eyes—"forty-eight hours."

Captain Sheridan looked anything but happy as he regarded the hugely shimmering mass of the Worm from Command and Control. To Ivanova he said, "I've called Earth Central and told them about this latest development; but, as before, they said they were already aware of it. This time, I didn't even bother to ask how they knew so quickly. It's obvious they have someone on Babylon 5 feeding them information."

"You're surprised at that?" Ivanova said wryly.

"No. But I am surprised that they don't care if I know or not. It's almost as if President Clark is flaunting the fact that Babylon 5 is not completely under our control."

Commander Ivanova said, "Captain, do you think Martina Coles could be a spy?"

"The thought had occurred to me. It's certainly possible. But even so, it doesn't explain how the transmissions are getting off Babylon 5 without our knowing about it."

"I've run scans, and as far as we can tell, no unauthorized transmissions have left Babylon 5 in the last twenty-four hours. But Martina is Psi Corps, Captain, and they seem to have their own way of doing things . . ."

"That they do."

"And she certainly dresses like a Psi Cop . . ." Ivanova looked at Sheridan expectantly.

Finally, the captain said, "All right, Commander.

Perhaps we should have Mr. Garibaldi keep an eye on her. But we *do* need her insights."

"Yes, unfortunately," Ivanova echoed.

Captain Sheridan studied the broad, twisted beauty of the Worm through the massive curved window.

"What *are* you?" he said, in a low voice, and Ivanova knew what he meant.

Lennier felt the oddest sensation he had ever felt in his life: he wanted to *strike* someone.

It was not totally unpleasant; certainly, there had been times in his life when frustration had overwhelmed common sense to the point where he felt there was no outlet. But to actually want to *hit* another being—well, that was a point he had never reached before.

It had happened out in the hallway, near his quarters; he had been returning from a brief meeting with Ambassador Delenn, his superior, when a short, intense woman dressed in black had brushed past him, and then moved on without making comment or apology.

Normally, Lennier would have been startled, and then immediately begun to analyze the situation: in a few moments it would have been forgotten, chalked up to experience. The experience: when people are in a great hurry, they sometimes run into innocent people and move on, because, in their minds, their mission is more important than those they bump into. Lesson learned.

But this time, Lennier had become instantly filled

with the same kind of indignation that Centauri, for example, seemed to evidence all the time—and he had wanted to chase after the woman, grab her by the shoulder, turn her around, and punch the woman in the face!

The feeling had been so startling that Lennier had immediately made his way to his quarters, made sure the door was closed behind him, and then began to analyze his reaction.

But his face, he saw in a mirror on the wall, was still flushed with anger! His fists were clenched with rage!

How odd! What to do?

He thought of returning to consult with Delenn, but knew that the ambassador was very busy with other matters.

He would have to figure this one out on his own.

And then—of course! The recent dreams! Where he ran amok in the hallways of Babylon 5, clad only in an ancient loincloth, armed with an Earth spear. They were startling, debilitating dreams, especially since in them he had acted with violence toward any non-Minbari he had met.

But that was the land of dreams—and this was reality.

In the mirror, his hands still had not unclenched; in his mind, the angry feeling over the slight he had received had not receded, as it should, but stood out in bold relief, gnawing at him.

For a brief moment, he wanted to search for a weapon and rush back out into the hallway, chasing down the woman and striking her—

Letting out an uncharacteristic howl, as much in surprise as in pain over his thoughts—he drove his fist into the mirror, shattering it and cutting his hand.

Almost instantly, his feelings of anger dissipated, as he studied the curious flow of blood across his knuckles, and the deeper gash across his wrist where a bright gush of blood was now pushing up, spilling over onto the floor.

Anger was gone; fear and disgust replaced it.

What have I done?

What am I now capable of doing?

These were terrible thoughts—new and terrible and frightening.

He watched the spill of blood; and then suddenly he realized that there really was a *lot* of blood, and that he should do something about it.

He called out for help, not knowing, as his legs weakened and he dropped to the floor, if he had succeeded or not.

He almost feared unconsciousness, not knowing what waited for him there.

But now it claimed him; and its dreams with it.

CHAPTER 11

DR. Stephen Franklin had his hands full.

Of course, there was the usual, routine business to attend to: the sprains, the industrial accidents (a particularly nasty eye operation on a Narn this morning: the fellow had gotten inattentive and fallen on his own tool while attempting to repair a lighting fixture in his quarters), the always-present common cold.

But now there was a whole other department of pain which the doctor had begun to log into Medlab, which Franklin had begun to register under the heading of "the Worm."

The doctor had no doubt that the Worm's roll call of death and mayhem had begun, and that it would continue to grow. As had Franklin's own frustration at not being able to discover any medical reason for the psychological affliction that seemed to be causing these new medical emergencies: namely, the nightmares.

Every spare moment away from the operating table and medicine cabinets had been spent in experimentation. With no time for sleep—and who'd want to, with these nightmares—he'd been relying on stims to keep him going. And so far, nothing. Just as the Worm seemed not to physically exist in space, so too did the nightmares seem to have no source. There was nothing wrong with any of the brains, human or alien, he had examined and scanned; it was as if a mass psychosis had taken hold of Babylon 5 in its entirety.

Which scared Franklin more than any disease, because he could fight a disease.

How do you fight something that isn't there?

Dr. Franklin was putting the final touches on his treatment of the Minbari Lennier when Garibaldi entered the Medlab.

"Looks like Grand Central Station in here, Doc," the security chief said.

"Something like that," Franklin agreed. He nodded down at the still unconscious Lennier. "It's not the quantity of the patients I'm worried about, but the quality."

Garibaldi studied Lennier's wrist. "Cut himself shaving?"

"Put his hand through a mirror. In anger, I suspect."

"Angry? Him?" Garibaldi gave a mock shudder. "He should be worried, now."

"How do you mean?" Franklin asked.

"Seven years' bad luck," Garibaldi said.

On his rounds, Garibaldi saw almost nothing but chaos now. He'd even gotten to the point where he had to release his own two miscreant security officers, Martin and Kristian, not because he wanted to, but because he needed them. There just weren't enough officers to go around. On every level, everywhere there was interaction between different species on Babylon 5—which was, of course, everywhere—there was trouble. Everything from minor skirmishes, fistfights, to near warfare which put them into Dr. Franklin's care.

Almost with relief, Garibaldi left Medlab—all those mained bodies in there were, in a way, the result of his failures as security chief—and headed to what he hoped would be a quieter section of Babylon 5. It was time for a little spying mission—something he enjoyed even more than security.

There was no response at Martina Coles's door. After waiting a reasonable amount of time, and checking that he was thankfully alone in the corridor, Garibaldi was about to, basically, break into the room when the door slid open on its own.

The petite, black-clad form of Martina Coles stood regarding him coldly.

"Were you about to break into my quarters?" she asked.

"As a matter of fact I was," Garibaldi answered,

moving past her to enter the quarters. "Actually, I'm one of the very few people aboard the station who can do that—if the situation warrants it."

"And how does the situation warrant it?" Martina said icily.

"Well," Garibaldi answered, glancing around the room as he spoke, "it's like this. I'm the security chief of Babylon 5, and at the moment we have a security problem. And you, I'm afraid, may be part of the problem." He smiled, looking at her evenly. "Would you like to be part of the solution?"

"I don't know what you're talking about. Please leave."

"I don't think so," Garibaldi said, all thoughts of subtlety abandoning him. "I just need to ask you a few questions."

Standing straight, Martina folded her arms.

"All right. Ask. Then get out."

"Tsk, tsk," Garibaldi scolded. "You're supposed to be on our side, remember? And anyway, you have a contract with Babylon 5, right?"

"That was not my doing."

"Is it ever? You people are just contract players, aren't you? I mean, the last contract player we had in here, lady by the name of Talia Winters, turned out to be a plant, and not a nice lady at all. How 'bout you? You a plant, too?"

"I didn't even want this assignment. I'm on my way to Omega Sector."

"Sure you are. But it's a little funny that you showed up just when we started having head problems on Babylon 5. Don't you think that's funny?"

When Martina said nothing, only regarded him tight-lipped, Garibaldi added, "Don't you?"

Martina continued to stare at him stonily; but Garibaldi had the feeling that her attention wasn't solely on him. She seemed to be fighting something. At first the security chief thought there might be someone else in the room, but then he realized that it was herself that she was fighting. She began to tremble, forcing back tears.

"Please . . . leave," she managed to get out.

"Hey . . ." Garibaldi said, suddenly concerned. "What's wrong? Can I help?"

A sob escaped her, and then she suddenly collapsed to the floor.

"What the—" Garibaldi rushed to her. She was out cold.

Carefully, the security chief lifted her body, which was light as a sack of feathers, and lay her on the bed. He looked down at her for a moment.

"Was it something I said?" he asked.

Then, rubbing his hands, he began to search the entire quarters, top to bottom, looking for any kind of transmission equipment or anything else at all incriminating.

The quarters were clean.

"Well, lady," he said, looking down at the telepath, who had begun to stir, "looks like you're off my hit list, at least for now."

He shook her shoulder. "Hey! Are you okay?"

Martina's eyes flew open and she stiffened, pushing herself up into a sitting position. "Please leave me alone," she said, refusing to look at him any further.

"Hey, I was just trying to help."

"I'm sure you helped yourself to searching my apartment while I was unconscious," she said.

"As a matter of fact I did."

"Good. Then leave."

"Not until you tell me why you fainted."

"It . . . happens to me."

Garibaldi was silent for a moment. "Sure it wasn't something else? Someone trying to crawl into your head? Like . . . maybe the Worm?"

"No!" she protested, a little too quickly. But Garibaldi could see real fear pass across her features. "I—"

"Yes?"

Martina took a long, shivering breath. "I . . . brushed against a young Minbari male after leaving Captain Sheridan's meeting in the briefing room. His emotions were very intense. By accident, I . . . read him."

"And?"

"This is difficult for me, because I do not read aliens."

Garibaldi waited patiently.

She took another shuddering breath. "I . . . sensed *extreme* hostility. Dangerous hostility, just below the surface. It had been dredged up from a very deep place. You remember the fear I spoke of in the meeting?"

"Yes."

"I think this Minbari male would not, under normal circumstances, even think of harming anyone. It is not in his nature. But this fear in him of others is about to get loose. And if that can happen in someone normally so peaceful . . ."

"Then we've got really big trouble coming on Babylon 5," Garibaldi said.

"Yes." The strain of what she had said was evident on her face. "Please, just leave me now."

"All right," the security chief said. He made as if to leave, then stopped and added, "If there's anything you ever want to talk to me about, just call."

She was silent, staring down, but then she nodded quickly. "Thank you," she said, in a small yet icy voice.

CHAPTER 12

In Captain Sheridan's office, Garibaldi said, "So that's all I got."

Sheridan nodded. "Then she knows something, but is either too frightened to tell us—or has been ordered not to."

Garibaldi said, "I have a feeling it's the former."

"For the time being we'll go with your feeling. But if she knows something about the Worm, I want to know what it is."

Garibaldi nodded. "And for the time being, there aren't any riots in progress on Babylon 5. But I have to tell you that my security forces are stretched to the limit. Some of my people haven't slept in thirty-six hours, and have been doing double and even triple shifts. We're like a balloon about to burst."

Sheridan said, "Good analogy. And I wish I could tell you that help was on the way, but it's not. Earth Central has been very vague. The most truth I could get out of them is that there aren't any Earthforce troops who could get here in time before the Worm reaches us." Sheridan smiled tiredly. "I've gotten pretty good at reading between the lines of what Earth Central says, and I get the feeling they're in as much of an uproar over the Worm as we are. They have no idea what it is, or what it could be, and it scares the hell out of them."

"But they don't have to meet it face-to-face in less than two days," Garibaldi said.

"No, they don't," Sheridan answered. "But we do."

The captain's link sounded.

"Captain?" came Ivanova's voice. "We're ready to send that probe out. Care to watch?"

"We'll be right there," Sheridan said, and both he and Garibaldi were already out of their chairs.

From Commander Ivanova's data screen at Command and Control, she and Sheridan and Garibaldi watched as the techs readied a sci-probe for deployment. It was one of their biggest models, and modifications had been made.

"There are a couple of scanners that we added to the package," Ivanova explained. "They're nothing more than what we use on Babylon 5, but we tweaked the tolerances so that, in close proximity to the Worm, they'll be more sensitive. In other words, we might pick up something with this that we couldn't scanning from Babylon 5."

In the launch bay, one of the techs gave Ivanova a high sign, and then all of the techs left the area.

Ivanova changed screen views, and now the glowing green ribbon of the Worm filled their sight.

"Ready?" Commander Ivanova said.

"I'm always ready," Garibaldi cracked.

Ivanova said, "Launch," and now a tiny point of light became visible in the lower section of the screen, curving up and away to compensate for the force exerted on it by Babylon 5's rotation; in a few moments, after tiny flashes from its thrusters, it was moving deliberately out toward the Worm.

"How long before the probe reaches it?" Captain Sheridan asked.

"With maximum thrusters, in five hours."

Sheridan studied the tiny point of light. "Let me know," he ordered.

"Of course, sir," Ivanova replied.

"And just in case, ready another probe with the same instrumentation."

"I will," the commander said.

Five hours later, the same triumvirate was gathered around Commander Ivanova's screen. The tiny point of light had long since become invisible against the glowing ribbon of green. Only the data flowing across the adjacent screen told Ivanova what she needed to know.

"Will we get visual from this?" Captain Sheridan asked.

"Yes," Ivanova said. "But only on closest approach. I thought we'd like to see if that green band was made up of discernible particles or not."

"If it doesn't work, we'll find out in forty hours," Garibaldi said.

Ivanova studied her data screen intently. "Two minutes to rendezvous, and still I get nothing but dimensional data. The probe is telling us that the Worm . . . is nine point two million miles long and five hundred and twenty-two thousand miles wide. That's it."

Sheridan hit his palm with his fist. "There has to be more to it than that."

"You would think so," Ivanova said.

Garibaldi, half in jest, said, "You have any weaponry on that probe?"

Ivanova said, "No."

"Too bad," Garibaldi said. "We could have zapped it, seen if we could get a little rise out of it."

"That's something to keep in mind for the future," Captain Sheridan said.

"Are you serious?" Garibaldi said.

"Completely," the captain answered. "That thing is heading for my station, and I want to know what it is. There would be nothing wrong with sending a little mosquito to bite the lion."

"I'll see what I can do," Ivanova said, her eyes once more studying the data.

"A half minute 'til visual," she said.

"Anything else to report?" Captain Sheridan asked.

"Nothing. We packed this probe with every scanner we could ram into it, but nothing's showing. Not in any wavelength. And it's not showing anything organic."

"What is it?" Sheridan said.

"Maybe in a moment we'll know . . ." Ivanova said; and then she added, "Visual in five seconds . . . four . . . three . . . two . . . one . . . *mark.*"

The screen beside the data flow blinked on, showing a rich starfield: the blackness of space peppered with pinpoints of stars.

"Where is it?" Garibaldi asked.

Ivanova, frowning, studied the data screen. "According to our instruments, you're looking at it."

"Could it be that the particles are so far apart that we're literally staring between them?" Captain Sheridan asked.

"Let me see," Ivanova said. After a command, the camera view pulled back and spread out, showing the same starfield, expanded.

"How come we can see it but the cameras can't?" Garibaldi said, looking up from the screen to look out through the curving window at the green band of light.

"Good question," Ivanova said, distractedly. "In a minute, the probe will be passing through the Worm."

"Which it can measure, but can't see?" Captain Sheridan asked, as the visual screen scanned a variety of color bands and magnifications.

"That's right. I've just put the cameras through every dance they know, and they pick up nothing in ultraviolet, infrared, the works."

The screen view steadied on the original sight now: a velvet blackness sprinkled with stars.

Ivanova started another countdown.

"Five seconds to path crossing," she said, eyes fixed on her data. "Four . . . three . . . two . . ."

Sheridan and Garibaldi stared fixedly at the visual screen.

"One . . . *mark.*"

Ivanova took her eyes from the data and looked at the screen.

"See anything?" she asked.

Garibaldi pointed to a corner of the screen.

"There are eight stars over there that look like a giraffe, if you play connect the dots," he said.

Captain Sheridan stood up straight. Anger flared on his face. "I've had just about enough of your levity, Garibaldi," he growled.

Garibaldi's eyes locked with the captain's, and he found himself filling with rage. As his hands balled into fists, Commander Ivanova stepped between Garibaldi and the captain and said, "I think you two are in bad need of rest." She turned to Captain Sheridan. "How long has it been since you slept?"

Abruptly, anger turned to tiredness on Sheridan's face. "Too long. I agree."

Garibaldi's rage deflated as suddenly as it had come on, and he turned away in embarrassment. "Sorry, Captain."

"There's nothing to be sorry about. We're tired, and we're being affected like everyone else." To Ivanova he said, "In the meantime, prepare another probe for launch. Only this time I want a weapon on board. Nothing fancy, and nothing that could possibly do more than stun that thing out there. I want to give the Worm the mosquito bite I mentioned."

"I just hope we can," Ivanova said.

CHAPTER 13

THE Trinocular Film Festival had continued, unabated, through all the recent trouble. After all, the Trivorians had waited almost five years for this event, and were very proud that it was being held on Babylon 5. They had had smaller festivals in the past, on Trivorian, but the number of cineasts on Trivorian was limited, and the Trivorians had hoped to share their budding film art with a wider audience. Also, they hoped to make a lot of credits in the bargain.

So nothing—especially not something as insubstantial as a phantom Worm or a rash of nightmares—was going to interfere with their conference.

Especially since they had been guileless enough

(some said, stupid) to put a refund clause on their tickets.

T. Tato, president of the Trivorian Film Society and Chairman of the Film Festival, was presently making a plea from the festival's auditorium stage. Already today half the seats remained empty, even though one of the festival's highlights was the experimental film, *Cloud,* in which the great avant-garde filmmaker T. Too had immersed himself in the stratosphere of Trivorian for a week, filming the formation and dissolution of clouds literally around him. That in itself was a great feat—but, as with all of Too's work, the art had occurred in the editing room, where Too had turned these clouds into metaphors for life and death, their first fetal puffings leading through maturity and then, inevitably, to the grave. On first viewing the film T. Tato himself had cried, a not-common event for a Trivorian, and a dangerous one, since the Trivorian's three eyes, large as saucers and arranged with one below and centered between the other two, produced a prodigious amount of tears. Indeed, the third, lower, eye was in grave danger from any sort of weeping, as it tended to get inundated with Trivorian tears, which were extremely brackish and corrosive.

The sight of a Trivorian wearing a patch on that third eye was almost always a sure sign that the wearer was a sensitive soul—and, in his younger days, T. Tato himself affected to wear one, though there had been nothing wrong with his eye.

But to the present problem—and it was a large one.

T. Tato stood on the auditorium's stage, begging for calm.

"The great Too's greatest work is about to commence!" he called out, into the rambunctious crowd. The crowd was a mixture today, half Trivorian and half other species, most of which required the special headsets that turned binocular into trinocular vision. At present these headsets, which were rather bulky and heavy, were being used as weapons.

"Please!" T. Tato implored, holding all three of his hands out. "I beg you to sit down. What is about to follow is perhaps the highlight of the festival!"

Out in the audience, a Trivorian was beaned by a flying headset, and went down in a swoon.

Moaning in agitation, and fearful now that the Festival, which had taken so long to plan, and on which so much was riding, would end in chaos and failure (and insolvency), T. Tato made a desperate motion to the projectionist in his high booth at the back of the auditorium.

"Start the show! Start the show!" he cried, as a headset flew by his own head.

Amid the uproar, the lights went out, and *Clouds* began.

While the titles ran, the uproar continued; but as the film began in earnest, quiet magically descended on the audience. The rioters sat in the nearest seat, fumbling on the ground for discarded headsets which they donned. On the triple screen, soft music swelled as a puff of water vapor, tinged with the dash of yellow sulphur in Trivorian's atmosphere, swirled from next to nothing to build and build in a graceful dance, until it had become mighty as a mountain in the yellow sky.

"Hurrah!" someone from the audience—a Trivorian—cried.

"Be quiet!" a Narn, not familiar with the Trivorian custom of showing approval during a film, shouted in answer.

"You're showing your ignorance!" an unwise Trivorian scolded the Narn.

"I'll show you, ignorant!" a second Narn said, removing his headpiece and flinging it at the Trivorian.

"Quiet down front!" a Centauri in the back row demanded; on being ignored he stood up and punched the audience member next to him, who then punched a third.

T. Tato, in a panic, climbed up onto the stage and called for quiet, even as the film continued to run on the three screens behind him.

"Please! Let us enjoy the art form!"

"It stinks!" someone in the audience called out, above even the rest of the uproar, and now what had been a violent disagreement became a riot.

When it was over, nearly an hour later, T. Tato sat amidst the ruins of the theater, dazed. Small curls of smoke rose from seats that had been set afire and then doused by security forces; there were piles of other seats which had been removed from their moorings and stacked to one side. Someone had even partly succeeded in destroying the specially constructed seat of the film critic from the planet Cotswold: the tank, which had contained five hundred gallons of water in which the critic had floated, had been smashed on one end, necessitating the emergency removal of the critic, who would not, T. Tato knew, be kind. T. Tato himself had been assaulted with Trinocular headsets, which covered his three arms and three legs like warts and were stacked painfully atop his head. In one hand he held the refund stubs of nearly a hundred Film Festival tickets; another hundred or so lay scattered about him.

"Ohhh, my," T. Tato moaned.

"I'm afraid your troubles aren't over, bub," Garibaldi said, standing astride T. Tato while he made notes. "Your people will have to pay for all the damage."

"Oh my!" T. Tato complained. "We'll never be able to do something like this again. A dream is dashed!"

Garibaldi nodded sympathetically while he wrote.

"Three chandeliers," Garibaldi muttered, making a list of damaged goods, "one trinocular movie screen, custom-made, one trinocular projector . . ."

"Ohhhh, myyyyyyy!" T. Tato said. "They even ruined the projector?"

"You bet they did," Garibaldi said. "Threw it out of the booth, and the projectionist after it. He's suing you, by the way. I hope your insurance is paid up."

"Insurance! Ohhhhhhh!"

While T. Tato wailed, Garibaldi gently lifted one of the trinocular headsets from the festival promoter's head and tried it on.

"Hey," Garibaldi asked, staring at the remains of the triple screen through the headset, "any chance you could run that *Clouds* flick? I heard it was great."

T. Tato only wept, not caring if his third, lower eye was damaged or not by his tears; perhaps an eye patch would be his badge of courage, now.

CHAPTER 14

FITFULLY, Captain Sheridan slept. And instantly, the dream he had been avoiding since last he had been able to sleep came to him.

He was in a darkened place. He knew he was inside, but didn't know what he was inside of. He reached down to touch the floor, and felt cold and damp beneath his fingers. The air around him was cold and damp, too.

He stood, and slowly, like a blind man, moved ahead, hands out in front.

Suddenly he reached a wall, cold and damp as the rest of his surroundings; he turned one way and found another wall; turned the opposite way and began to make his way along the wall.

Sensing that he was now in a hallway, he reached out to either side and discovered that this was true.

Up ahead, there was the faintest light.

He continued, cautiously. The light faded, then came back stronger, outlining a doorway.

When Sheridan reached it he found a closed door, with illumination beyond.

Feeling around the door with his fingers, he found no way to open it.

Abruptly, the door slid back, opening.

He was blinded, and shielded his eyes with his arm. He hesitated, seeking to let his eyes adjust to the light, which they slowly did.

"Captain Sheridan, come in, please."

He did not know the voice, but it was one of command. He uncovered his eyes, trying to see the speaker, but there was only light.

Cautiously, he took a step, then another.

Behind him, the door closed.

"Captain, please."

"I can't see you!" Sheridan said.

"It is not necessary for you to see us, now. Come forward, please."

Sheridan obeyed, until the voice said, "Stop."

He stood, again trying to peer through the light.

He heard a murmur of voices now.

"He is not worthy," one said.

Another said, "He will never be worthy."

"He fought in the war," a third said.

"True," the original voice said. Then it said to Sheridan, "You may look upon us, now."

The intensity of the light went down, to the point

where Captain Sheridan could discern the outlines of figures. The figures were still bathed in light.

"I . . . still can't see who you are," Sheridan said.

Then another voice, one he thought he knew, said, "Let him see."

Again the light diminished, and now Captain Sheridan's blindness left him. He saw nine figures standing in a circle around him, wearing grey cloaks; they were Minbari, with triangles on their foreheads.

"You're . . . the Grey Council?" Sheridan asked, turning slowly to look at each in turn. He could not quite make out their features.

"Yes," one of the figures answered, the first who had addressed him. Sheridan stopped before him.

"What do you want from me?" he asked.

"The question is, what is it that you fear?"

"I don't understand," Sheridan said.

"When our two peoples went to war, it was because of fear. It is known that a man cannot conquer his fear until he knows what it is. I ask you again, Captain Sheridan: what is it that you fear?"

"I don't know how to answer that."

"Perhaps you do."

One of the other grey-cloaked figures approached Sheridan from behind, breaking the circle, and put a hand on his shoulder.

John Sheridan turned and looked into Ambassador Delenn's eyes.

"Do you fear me, Captain?" she asked directly.

"No, I . . . don't think so."

"He does not know himself," one of the others said simply. "He knows nothing about himself."

"This may be true," another said.

"Perhaps, then, he will learn."

Instantly, it became dark again, and John Sheridan felt cold dampness close in around him.

"Where are you!" he called. "Come back!"

His words were swallowed by darkness.

Again he put his fingers to the floor, and found that he was back where he had started.

He moved forward, until once again he reached the wall.

He turned right and found another wall; turned left and began to walk, once more, down the darkened hallway.

At the end was an outline of light, which grew as he approached, not into a doorway but a panel set into the wall; around it shone its outline.

He felt the panel, found a slot on one side and tried to slide it back.

It would not move.

Bringing his face close to it, he tried to find another way of opening the panel.

Behind the panel he heard Delenn's voice, and those of the members of the Grey Council.

Suddenly, the panel flew back, revealing a lit mirror, into which Captain John Sheridan stared.

He saw his own face—and he was Minbari.

CHAPTER 15

AGAIN, Martina Coles felt an alien presence in her mind.

And, once again, she tried to fight it off.

This was not the Vorlon, Kosh, come for a return visit. So far, Kosh had respected her wish that he stay away from her. At least, she knew, the Vorlon felt that she was not "ready" for his counsel—the thought of which made her shiver. If it was within her power, she would never be ready to read the Vorlon, or any other alien.

Including this one, which invaded her mind.

It was, she knew, the Other, the thing that existed and yet did not exist, the thing outside Babylon 5. The Worm. She knew it was, just as she knew that her fingers were on her hand, and her eyes stared out from her own head.

Stay away from me, she ordered it; but it was as if she had not spoken. It was . . . there. She wondered if it was even aware of her.

But there it was, at the back of her mind, like an insistent hum that wouldn't go away.

"Stay away from me!" she shouted, out loud, and knew that she was in danger of fragmenting. Every time she tried to sleep the horrible dreams came—and when she was awake, the insistent hum was there, pushing at her, pushing . . .

With a wail of pain, Martina fell to her knees, holding her head.

"Just . . . go . . . away . . ." she sobbed, but the thing was there, the Worm, insistent . . .

Still sobbing, she crawled to her bed and lay down, begging for sleep. Even dreams were better than this.

She closed her eyes.

And her dream came . . .

It was not so much a dream as a memory, dredged up from the deepest recesses of her mind. She had buried it there long ago, in a place that no one could find, not even Psi Corps.

Yes, not even Psi Corps had been able to open that locked box, in that faraway corner of Martina Coles's deepest mind, where she hid her darkest secret.

She had just passed the age of sixteen. She had not seen her parents since she had been taken under the wing of Psi Corps, and now, she was told, she was to have a very special visitor.

Blooming with hope, she had thought that her parents might be allowed to visit her. But when she was left alone at the door to the conference room, and then went in and closed it behind her, she found not her mother and father, who even now were fading memories, but someone else.

A figure stood at the window with its back to her, hands clasped. The room was plushly outfitted, with club chairs and a sofa; the windows were heavily draped.

Just the sight of those hands, spotted brown and reptilian, told her instantly that she was in the presence of an alien. She had never seen an alien before—had not been in the presence of anyone outside of Psi Corps for seven years—and here was a real live alien, as if it had jumped off a page of a book. She had learned about the various races, of course, as part of her training—but here was the real thing.

Before it turned around she knew that it was a Narn. The distinctive reptilian features told her that. But she was startled when it did turn around: for, apparently, it was of an age similar to her own—and male.

The Narn blinked, standing stiff as it regarded her, hands still held behind its back.

"I am . . . N'Teth," it said, bowing slightly.

Diplomacy and etiquette were of course part of Psi Corps training, and Martina bowed slightly also. "My name is Martina Coles."

"Mar . . . tina," the Narn said, sampling her first name as if it was a delicacy. It nodded once, approvingly. "I like it."

Martina withheld an urge to be sarcastic and said merely, "Thank you."

"Would you . . . like to sit?" N'Teth asked, removing one hand from behind its back to indicate the sofa.

Martina said, "Certainly."

She sat politely on one end of the couch; but, to her surprise, the Narn sat right next to her. He cocked his head, looking at her curiously.

"You are not . . . what I expected," he said.

"And you expected . . . ?" Martina asked.

"Someone . . . taller. More . . ." He shrugged. "Robust."

She could not help smiling. "Robust?"

"Perhaps I wasn't clear," N'Teth said. "Perhaps . . . *stronger* is a better word."

Though she kept her equanimity, Martina smiled inwardly. Her self-defense classes made her more than confident that she could pin this Narn's back to the floor—or any three like him.

"I see . . ." she said.

"You do? Then you have been told?" N'Teth was studying her even more intently.

"Told what?" Martina asked.

But even as she said the words out loud, she knew what he meant.

His thoughts came at her as clear as any she had ever read. As he raised his hand slowly to touch her, she saw it all in his mind, and instantly shrank back.

"What's wrong?" he said, alarmed. "Did they not tell you any of it? They believe that a cross-breed, if possible, would yield an . . . offspring more powerful than anything Psi Corps has yet seen. The Narn government was of course appalled at the idea when it was discreetly proposed, but that did not stop Psi Corps from making their inquiries."

She saw it all in his mind: his incarceration for crimes committed against Narn women; his assisted escape—all of it. She saw the filthy thoughts that were going through his mind at the moment.

"We do not have to do it the traditional way, if you insist. Psi Corps would be more than willing to try an artificial birthing—though they would be more happy with this." He smiled stiffly, and managed to make it a leer. "And so would I, to tell you the truth. I have been rather looking forward to . . . trying the traditional method."

His hands were on her, stronger than she thought they would be. She was trapped in a corner of the couch, and began to protest.

"That is good! They . . . fight back on my world, also . . ."

Martina was able to escape with a flat hand to his face; as she fled she looked back from the doorway and saw him beginning to recover, his startled look being replaced by anger.

And so she ran, and ran . . .

She ran to the edge of the grounds, climbing to the top of a tree she knew there from her younger days. She thought of fleeing Psi Corps, but knew in the end they would find her, and bring her back into the fold.

Instead she decided to go back and be ever on her guard . . .

Nothing was ever said of N'Teth, nor was he ever seen again. The woman who had sent her to the room where the Narn had waited for her was gone the next day; it was as if it had never happened.

And so she pushed it down into a secret place, where it became a bad dream, and there she locked it away, along with her resolve never again to read an alien, never again to subject herself to the *filthy* thoughts in an alien mind . . .

She awoke, sobbing, and with the insistent hum of the Worm in her mind. She thought she was going mad. Her head felt as if it were in a vise—squeezed on one side by the Worm and on the other by the promise of horrible sleep. For such a sleep was no sleep at all.

What am I going to do?

And then, with much reluctance, she knew that there was only one course for her to take.

One course that might prevent her from going mad.

Kosh, she called out, tentatively, and then with insistence. *Kosh, I must speak with you. I think I'm ready.*

CHAPTER 16

"HAVE you been sleeping at all?" Dr. Franklin asked Commander Susan Ivanova, who stared too intently at her data screen in C&C.

"Susan, did you hear me?"

"Hmmm?" Commander Ivanova said.

"I said, have you been sleeping at all?"

"No, I haven't."

"I can tell," Dr. Franklin said. "Tell me: what are you looking at now?"

"I'm studying the readout of the second probe we're preparing. We're launching it in an hour."

"Tell me what you've just read on that screen."

"I can't," Ivanova said, pulling her eyes from the data to stare at Franklin. A tiny smile crossed her lips. "I can't because I've been staring at the screen like a zombie for fifteen minutes. I need a break."

She rubbed her eyes and yawned.

"You need more than that. Come with me."

Like a parent, Franklin took Ivanova's hand and drew her after him to the briefing room, where Captain Sheridan and Garibaldi were already waiting for them. Garibaldi had his head on the table, cradled in his arms.

"Fire at will!" he said groggily, lifting his head as the door closed behind Franklin and Ivanova.

"As all of you can see," Franklin said, "We have a real command problem on board Babylon 5. The problem is sleep deprivation. I guarantee that if the three of you go on the way you have been, this ship will be in total chaos by tomorrow. You won't have to go to sleep to have nightmares; there will be real ones and whatever isn't real you'll hallucinate into being."

"I agree," Captain Sheridan said. "Something has to be done."

"How come you look so chipper, Doc?" Garibaldi yawned.

"Not chipper, exactly. But I have just been able to grab three hours of uninterrupted sleep. I dreamed, and they were nightmares, the same I've been having about doing an autopsy on a dead Drazi only to have him come back to life and try to strangle me as I stood there holding his brain; but they were mild dreams and pushed to the background."

Captain Sheridan's interest was immediately piqued. "How did you manage to sleep that long?"

Franklin held up a huge pill between his thumb and forefinger. "A little something I came up with, in my spare time between setting broken arms and patching broken heads."

"My God," Garibaldi said, "what do you think we are—horses?"

Franklin smiled. "I tried to do this with an injection, but it wouldn't mix for me. The only way to take it is the good old-fashioned way—preferably with a glass of water."

Garibaldi said, "Hold the water and it'll get stuck in your throat and choke you!"

Franklin continued to smile.

"So what is it, Doc?" Captain Sheridan said.

"It's actually a mild sedative, and a mild opiate. The opiate handles the nightmares, taking the edge off them, while the sedative lets you get some deep REM sleep."

"That's great! Can we get enough for everyone on board?"

"That's the bad news, Captain. The opiate is tough to synthesize, and I'm afraid it will only work a few times before your body gets used to it and renders it ineffective. Then the nightmares will come back full force. But this will buy us some time."

"How much can you manufacture?"

"Only enough for command staff, and possibly a few of Garibaldi's security officers."

"Well, at least it will buy us some time!" Sheridan said enthusiastically.

Franklin nodded, and pulled a handful of pills from his pocket. He gave two each to the captain, Commander Ivanova, and Chief Garibaldi. "I suggest that you take one of these before you go to sleep. Do it in shifts, starting immediately." He looked at Commander Ivanova, who was holding her pills in her hand and looked about to faint.

"May I suggest that Commander Ivanova take hers first?"

Captain Sheridan said, "Of course." He shook Franklin's hand. "Great work, Doctor."

Franklin smiled. "And if you could get Mr. Garibaldi's men to do a better job of preventing the inhabitants on Babylon 5 from breaking each other's bones, I might have time to come up with something even better."

"Keep working when you can, Doctor."

"I'll do that," Franklin said. He pointed to Ivanova, who had sat down and was half asleep in her chair. "I think she'd have a much better sleep if you get one of those pills into her as soon as possible."

Garibaldi was already filling a glass with water from the carafe on the table.

"Time for sweet dreams," he said, holding the glass to Ivanova's lips, along with one of the horse pills.

After overseeing the launch of the second probe, Captain Sheridan was looking forward to his own rest period; he had just left the command console in the Observation Dome when his link sounded.

"Sheridan here."

"Captain, this is Garibaldi. I just ran into Ambassador Delenn, who looked very upset. She wouldn't tell me what's bothering her but she very much wants to talk to you. Sorry to do this to you, but I get a funny feeling this is important. She's waiting back in the briefing room now."

"That's all right, Chief. Why don't we switch rest periods? You take mine now, and I'll take mine in three hours."

"Oh, blessed sleep," Garibaldi said.

Sheridan joked, "You didn't manufacture this new crisis just so you could get to sleep before me, did you, Chief?"

"Me? Actually, I didn't think of it. Maybe next time . . ."

"Sheridan out."

Garibaldi hadn't been joking; Delenn looked as agitated as the captain had ever seen her. Part of it, he surmised, was due to lack of sleep; but there was definitely something bothering her.

"Delenn?" Sheridan sat across the table from her. "What's wrong?"

Delenn took a deep breath.

"You have not gotten official word from my government through yours, Captain, but you will before long. It seems my government has put my world on full alert."

"What!" Sheridan said, startled. "Why?"

"This Worm phenomenon. It is feared back home that it is a . . . trick. Perhaps as a prelude to war."

"But that's absurd! Neither of us knows more about this thing than the other!"

"Captain," Delenn said sadly, "you know that, and I know that. But we are dealing with governments here, and governments do not always . . . work by the same rules as reasonable people." She took another deep breath. "As of now, all Minbari warships have been put on highest alert. There . . . has been some talk of pulling me back to Minbari."

"That would be the worst thing that could happen! Babylon 5 is neutral ground, run jointly by both the Earth and Minbari! Pulling you back would be the first step toward a declaration of war!"

"I am resisting this with all of my power. But there is . . . a chance I may lose."

"Delenn, what can I do?"

"Talk to your own government, and assure them that these . . . actions are only precautions. Tell them that as far as I am concerned, this has nothing to do with our good relations. It is merely in . . . self-defense against the unknown."

"In other words, blame it on the Worm."

"Exactly. I am doing everything I can to make sure the Minbari declaration is couched in the same terms. In this, at least, I may be able to succeed. I will talk to my own government again in a few hours and tell them, with your blessing, that no matter what happens, Babylon 5 will remain neutral territory. In this way we can work to defuse this situation."

Delenn's eyes suddenly closed for a moment; she startled herself awake and held a hand over her mouth to stifle a yawn.

"I must get some rest before I talk to my people again," she said.

"Have you slept at all?"

She nodded. "A little. I . . . keep having that same horrible dream."

"The one where I try to kill you?"

"Yes," she said. Her eyes closed again briefly. "It is doubly horrible now, because it . . . seems a precursor . . ."

Sheridan made it around the table to catch her as she tilted over, half asleep.

"Delenn," Sheridan whispered.

She awoke and looked up into his eyes, smiling weakly.

"Hello, Captain."

Sheridan fished in his pocket and produced one of Dr. Franklin's pills. He activated his link and called Dr. Franklin.

"Doctor?" he asked. "Would it be safe for me to give Ambassador Delenn one of my pills?"

Without hesitation Franklin answered, "Yes. It will have the same effect on a Minbari system as on yours."

"Thank you, Doctor," Sheridan said. He pressed the pill into Delenn's hand.

"I'm going to help you back to your quarters, and then I want you to take this. It will help you sleep."

"Yes, Captain . . ." She nodded.

Realizing that she would never make it to her quarters, the captain poured a glass of water from the carafe on the table and prodded Delenn back from sleep long enough to get her to swallow the pill.

"Awful . . . pill . . ." she said, making a face.

Sheridan laughed. "Yes. But it will give you a restful sleep."

Her eyes locked on Sheridan's for a moment, before they fluttered back to sleep. "Could . . . never . . . kill you . . . Captain . . ."

Sheridan arranged her as comfortably as he could on the chair, and removed his jacket to place over her. He looked down at her as she slept, looking as peaceful as a child.

"And I could never kill you, Delenn," he whispered.

CHAPTER 17

GARIBALDI felt like a new man after his three-hour sleep period. The nightmare of crashing into an alien planet had still been there, but it had been muted: like watching something from far away.

But the rest of Babylon 5 hadn't had that three hours of restful sleep, and things were as wild as ever.

Good time to go underground, Garibaldi thought.

He retrieved what he liked to call his disguise: a fedora hat, private-eye-type coat, and comfortable shoes. He had worn this before, once when looking for a fugitive in Brown sector with Dr. Franklin.

He was looking for a fugitive once again: a fugitive transmitter.

Scanning had indicated that unlawful transmissions were being made from within Babylon 5 itself—and that they were coming from somewhere Down Below.

To Garibaldi, it made sense that this might be the transmitter alerting Earth Central to everything happening on board Babylon 5—in other words, find the transmitter and you find the spy.

Garibaldi's first stop was the Wet Rock, a beer shack where the greasy food was even worse than the suds.

He walked into the middle of a fight.

A body flew past him, grunting as it hit a table flush on the top, breaking it.

"Oh, great," Garibaldi said. "Here we go again."

He caught the next body as it flew at him, and found himself supporting a drunk human, who tried to flail away from him. He knew the guy—he was a cargo bay worker who had once—surprise—gotten drunk and started a fight.

"All right, Lauro—what seems to be the problem?" Garibaldi said into the drunk man's ear.

"Lemme go! Lemme!" Lauro said, pinwheeling his arms and trying to get back into the fray, which seemed to have taken over one corner of the Wet Rock: there was a group of humans surrounding a very mad Narn, and the humans were periodically being hurled off in various directions.

"That . . . Narn told us we were no good!"

"You probably aren't," Garibaldi said, bearing the man to the nearest table, picking a chair up from the floor, and setting Lauro down on it.

"Time to talk, Lauro," Garibaldi said.

"Hey, you're . . ." Lauro said, trying to focus on Garibaldi.

"That's right. And unless you want to spend some more time behind bars, I think your lips should start saying things I want to hear."

They were interrupted by another body sliding past on the floor.

Garibaldi turned to watch it slide completely under a table.

"Score!" Garibaldi said, turning back to Lauro, who was trying to fall asleep.

"Wake up," Garibaldi said, pushing at him.

"Huh?" Lauro said, focusing again on Garibaldi. "Oh, yeah. Whaddaya wanna know?"

"I'm looking for a transmitter. An illegal one."

"Don' know nutthin'. Just tired, is all. And sleepy. Want to sleep but don' wanna dream. Y'know?"

"Yeah, I know," Garibaldi said. "But what I really want to know is where I can find a transmitter down here."

"Talk t' Harry."

"Harry? Harry who?"

"Harry . . ."

Lauro started to nod off; but another human flew into him from behind, startling him awake.

"Stay away from me, damn alien!" Lauro shouted, coming out of his dreams.

Garibaldi reached across the table and took the bay worker by the shirt.

"Tell me Harry's last name," he said.

"Harry? Why, Harry Chase, of course."

Lauro went slack in Garibaldi's grip, and as the security chief lowered his upper body to the table Lauro began to snore.

"Get away . . . alien . . ." Lauro mumbled.

Garibaldi got up, stepping nimbly over another body which slid across the floor, disappearing beneath the same table as the first; there was a grunt of surprise and then snoring silence.

Garibaldi looked at the continuing melee in the corner, thought of stopping it but merely shrugged and walked out.

Harry Chase was somebody he could find.

Chase had a shop in the deepest part of Down Below. It was dangerous in there—everybody knew that—but Chase liked it that way. That was because only really serious clients would come to see him—and that was the way Chase liked that, too.

Harry Chase was a careful, smart man. Some said he had worked on Blacklight Camouflage, the electronic shielding developed by Earthforce which effectively bent light around objects, rendering them all but invisible. Some said he had done other things for Earthforce, an even more black project than that. Garibaldi tended to doubt those stories, mostly because the origins of these rumors always traced back directly to Harry Chase himself. He was a walking advertisement for himself—something no one so intimately involved in such high-tech business would do. It would be stupid, and dangerous, to do so.

But Harry was good at what he did, which was to

transfer certain electronics from one hand into the other. He was a fence, plain and simple—though Michael Garibaldi had never been able to catch him at it.

Garibaldi passed two interspecies fistfights, and three Lurkers beating on a fourth—who turned out to be a Drazi. Garibaldi chased them off with his badge.

He knocked on the ramshackle door that led to Chase's "parlor"—a junk-laden room with holes in the walls. When no one answered, Garibaldi pushed open the door and entered.

What met him was a surprise: the room was empty, stripped of every piece of equipment and gadget. There had been a tall pile of tech manuals in one corner, and even these were gone.

"Hey, Harry?" Garibaldi called, walking through the echoes that inhabited the room now.

There was a sound from the back of the place, through a door that led into darkness.

Garibaldi pulled his gun and proceeded.

"Harry Chase?" the security chief shouted. "This is Garibaldi! Come out with your hands up!"

Again came the rattling sound from the back, and, gun ready, Garibaldi went through the door into the dimness, ready for anything.

Sudden light blinded Garibaldi as a section of flimsy wall was pushed out as someone dived through it.

"Hey!" Garibaldi cried, diving after the figure who had thrown itself out into an adjoining alley.

Garibaldi felt his hands on shoes, which tried to

kick free of him. The security chief secured the thrashing form, raising his gun so that the figure could see it.

"Don't move," Garibaldi said.

The figure went still, moaning, "Oh no, oh no."

"Now turn over," Garibaldi said, relieving some of the pressure so that the figure beneath him could roll over onto its back.

It was a young girl with dirty hair—a Lurker.

"I din' mean nothin', man! Jus' lookin' fer food!"

"Where's Harry Chase?" Garibaldi said.

"Gone! Oh, please don' tell 'im I was casing his joint, mister! Please don'!"

"I won't," Garibaldi said, putting his weapon away. To the dirty-faced girl he said, "Do you know where Harry went?"

"Gone!" the girl said. "Getting out! Leaving!"

"You mean Harry's leaving Babylon 5?" Garibaldi said.

"You bet! Jus' like everybody else roun' here!"

Garibaldi knew that there were other black-market merchants in the area.

"You mean all the other shops? They're all closed?"

The girl nodded wildly.

"Why?" Garibaldi asked. "Why are they leaving?"

"Getting out!" the girl cried, wild-eyed. "Before the world ends!"

CHAPTER 18

"AND so my friends," said the Reverend Bobby James Galaxy, of the Universal Church of Solar Illumination, with passion, "we must face the coming ca-la-mi-ty with forthrightness! We must look the devil in the eye and tell him no! We must stand up on our own two feet—because that is the way that God made us, with two feet—and stare the evil down!"

"Amen!" came a fervent voice, amidst many other hosannas.

"Yes!" cried the Reverend Bobby, holding his hands out above his disciples in benediction. "You must understand that this is a battle of the ages! A battle for all time! That the coming battle will rid mankind of all the scourges that have been placed upon him! That once again man, in God's own image, will rule!"

The roar was deafening, and the ruined hall where the Trinocular Film Festival had taken place, which had been cleared out by the reverend's disciples so that they could hold a rally, shook to all its loosened girders with the sounds of the nearly thousand who had packed their way in.

A thousand faces from Earth—and not one alien among them.

"Let there be no mistake!" Reverend Bobby shouted with conviction, as he stood on the stage under the single screen which had not been damaged: on it was projected an image of the Worm, twisted and glowing softly green. The reverend pointed to it. "And let there be no denying the truth! The Age of Renewal is upon us! And here—here!—is our deliverer!"

The throng went wild, and the reverend had to wait nearly five minutes for them to quiet down. In the meantime, he made a motion to his Special Disciples, the twelve green-hooded men who flanked him, who began to fan out through the crowd, bearing baskets.

"Give! Give with your hearts and souls, my sisters and brothers! Give so that our work can continue—and the sign of the Worm will bear the fruit that we know is within it! Give so that we may drive the heathen from Babylon 5, and from the very Universe!"

A woman in front fainted; and another began to roll her eyes, waving her hands above her head as strange words in a strange tongue came from her mouth.

The reverend now descended the stairs and began to work his way into the crowd, laying his hands upon heads, kissing young ones. When credit chits were thrust into his hands he smiled beautifically and would not accept them; however, one of his Twelve immediately appeared and thrust a basket at the giver to accept the gift.

After working his way through the crowd the Reverend Bobby James Galaxy made his way slowly back up to the stage. Once again his green-robed disciples flanked him.

There were tears in his eyes. For a moment he turned to behold the vision of the Worm on the screen behind him. Then he suddenly put his face in his hands and wept.

There were gasps and weepings from the crowd, and someone shouted, "We love you, Reverend!"

"As I love you!" Reverend Bobby wailed, thrusting his hands out over them. His face glistened with tears, but there was a smile on his face: a smile of ecstasy.

"Join me now in prayer!"

All heads bowed; all eyes closed; the reverend's among them.

"O Lord, who is our Lord alone, please listen to our plea.

"For we have lived among the heathen too long, oh Lord. We have abandoned your words, and forsaken your teachings, and given ourselves up to the devils.

"But we repent our sins, and return our souls and our love to you. For we now know that man was made in your image alone; and that your image is not in those who do not bear our image. We are the chosen people, and no other.

"That, we now know; and that, we do now swear to uphold.

"Amen."

"AMEN!" resounded the chorus of a thousand voices.

Bobby James Galaxy held up his hands once more above them; in one of them was a PPG rifle. Drying tears still glistened on his cheeks.

"God bless you!" he shouted. And then he added, "When the time is right, let us take back the universe from the alien heathen!"

CHAPTER 19

"THIS is almost beyond belief."

Looking almost rested, Captain Sheridan paced from one end of the briefing room to the other. He could not believe what he was hearing

"You're telling me that the black marketers in Down Below are abandoning Babylon 5, because they think it's on the verge of destruction?"

"That's the scuttlebutt," Garibaldi reported. "I didn't find the transmitter I was looking for, but I visited five more places, including two chop shops dealing in stolen shuttle parts, after I left Harry Chase's place, and all of them were boarded up and abandoned."

"Rats leaving a sinking ship," Ivanova mumbled, instantly sorry she had said it.

Sheridan showed brief anger. "This *isn't* a sinking ship," he said. "But it is a bad sign." He turned all of his attention to the Commander. "And what have you learned about transport departures?"

Ivanova straightened in her chair. "They're up, as could be expected. But nothing approaching panic. I think what we're seeing is the first wave of something that could get worse."

"The rats always leave first," Garibaldi said, picking up on Ivanova's unfortunate comment.

"All right, how do we alleviate panic?" Sheridan said.

"We don't," Garibaldi said. "We merely try to control it."

"How?"

"By adding extra security to the docking bays, while at the same time keeping everything as normal as possible," Garibaldi answered. "If people want to leave they're going to leave, but like I said, we try to keep it orderly."

"All right," Sheridan said, "we'll do what you say. But have security keep a low profile. I don't want any panic."

Garibaldi nodded. "Agreed."

Ivanova nodded in agreement.

Sheridan said, "On to other business. Ivanova, what about the second scientific probe?"

The commander got a sour look on her face. "As useless as the first. We fired some low-level bursts at the Worm, and continued them all the way to the time when the probe passed through the spot where it should be. There was a video camera on board;

once again, it showed nothing. And there was no change in the Worm when it was hit."

"Did you learn anything else at all?"

Sheepishly, Ivanova shook her head.

"Okay," Sheridan said, "it's time to get more serious. I suggest we send a manned mission out to it."

"You mean Starfuries?" Ivanova asked, surprised.

"No, a shuttle mission. Packed to the hilt with every instrument we've got. I want your science team to come up with anything they can, any possible experiment that could shed some light on what we're dealing with. I imagine it's driving the physics boys nuts, am I right?"

Ivanova nodded vigorously. "You've got that right. There's a Dr. Laramie who's about to burst a blood vessel. The science team's been lobbying for a shuttle mission anyway, Captain. Should I set it up?"

"As soon as you can. I also want to see if Dr. Franklin's made any progress on that sleep pill. I can't think of anything else that would do more good at the moment." Captain Sheridan looked up. "Any other business?"

The captain's link chimed.

"Sheridan here," he said into it.

"This is Command and Control, Captain. I thought you should know that someone has launched a ship at the Worm."

"What?"

"Someone has launched—"

Impatiently, Sheridan said, "I'll be right there. Of what origin is it?"

"Centauri, Captain. We've scanned it, and it's armed to the teeth."

CHAPTER 20

In Command and Control, Captain Sheridan asked, "How long before that Centauri ship gets to the Worm?"

Ivanova, who had taken over the control console, said, "About three hours."

"And how many Centauri are on board?"

"Scanners tell us only one."

"It's not Londo, is it?"

Commander Ivanova answered, "The ambassador doesn't answer our calls."

Garibaldi piped in: "That doesn't mean anything. He only answers when he feels like it anyway."

Sheridan said, *"Damn."*

Garibaldi had a sudden thought.

"I . . . think I know where I might be able to find Londo."

The captain said, "Then by all means do so! I need to talk with him."

"I'll see what I can do, Captain."

Just as Garibaldi thought, he found the Centauri ambassador at the Zocolo, at the bar.

Londo looked like he had had more than one, and when he saw Garibaldi, he merely turned back to the bar and called for the bartender.

"Another of these—now, please!"

The bartender, busy with a big crowd, ignored him.

"There's no such thing as respect anymore!" Londo complained.

Garibaldi joined him and said, "What's wrong, Londo—lose a big bet?"

Londo turned to him angrily, then said in a restrained voice, "You could say that."

"Want to talk about it?"

"No." Then the ambassador said, sighing, "Actually, yes. As you know I am a betting man. And now it seems I have lost the wager of a lifetime." He raised his glass in front of Garibaldi. "I have bet, you see, my *career* on Babylon 5. And am about to lose it."

Garibaldi said, "How do you mean?"

Now the Centauri did sneer. "Are you *blind*? This station will no longer exist in thirty-six hours. Either that . . . *worm* will get it, or the crazies on board will rip it to shreds. I always thought Babylon 5 was a madhouse—and now I am sure of it."

"You really think this will destroy us?"

"Anyone can see that. And along with it will go everything I've worked for."

"Taking the long view, eh, Londo?"

With a grain of apology, Londo said, "You know what I mean, Garibaldi. Look at your own security forces. They look like . . . what is your word . . . *zombies.* The walking dead. Working on little sleep and nightmares."

Garibaldi said, "Have you been having your own nightmares, Londo?"

"Have I! Like every bad dream I ever had as a boy rolled up into one. Offworlders under the bed, foreigners in the closet, Minbari in the cellar . . ."

He shook his head, then took another drink and held up the glass.

"*This* is the only thing that has kept me going, my friend."

Without raising his voice, Garibaldi asked, "Londo, did you send that Centauri ship out to the Worm?"

"Of course I did! What else could I do! If I can blast that horrid thing out of the sky I'll save my career! Be a hero here and at home!" He turned and smiled at Garibaldi. "Why, my friend, I even did it for you!"

"Would you do something else for me, Londo?" Garibaldi asked mildly, steering the drunken diplomat away from the bar.

"Of course, Garibaldi! Anything you want! As long as I can have a drink!"

Garibaldi smiled. "Good. Come with me."

* * *

An hour later, as Sheridan and Commander Ivanova watched from the control console, the Centauri ship settled back into its bay, the docking grapples grabbing it tightly. Sheridan turned to Garibaldi.

"I can't believe you were able to get Londo to turn that ship around so easily."

Garibaldi said, "You can thank me, and a little pure grain alcohol I fed him after the ten or so drinks he already had in him. I think I could have talked him into stripping down to his Skivvies and putting on a hula skirt."

Ivanova made a face. *"There's* an image."

Captain Sheridan said, "This episode does bring up an interesting point. We'll have to have the Advisory Council involved when we send out our own probe. I think that would be prudent, and fair."

"Including the League of Non-Aligned Worlds?"

"Especially them. I think that would be the smart move, getting as many inhabitants of Babylon 5 as possible involved in the process. We seem to have nothing but fragmentation going on. I'd like to try to go the other way a little bit. And, in the face of what we just went through, I think we should get that mission together as soon as possible."

"Should we convene a meeting?" Ivanova asked.

"Yes," Sheridan answered. "Make it for . . . two hours from now."

"We're running out of time," Ivanova declared.

"I know," Sheridan answered.

CHAPTER 21

It is time for you to see me.

Kosh's words burned in her mind, but still she refused to listen to them.

"No, I won't. I've changed my mind. Leave me alone!"

But it is time. You are ready.

"I'll never be ready!"

Come . . .

Curled on her bed in a fetal position, eyes shut tightly, Martina Coles felt as if she were about to be torn apart. There was sanctuary neither in sleeping nor in wakefulness. Demons waited for her in both.

Aliens.

Again Kosh's words came, pushing in front of the insistent buzz that the Worm exerted on her.

There will be no other time.

"I cannot see you!"

Come . . .

A sob escaped her. Slowly she uncurled from the bed, afraid that she would break apart. She put her feet gently to the floor, concentrating on the act to block out the noises in her mind.

Good. You are coming.

She avoided a mirror on the wall, not looking at the haunted being reflected in its silver. She moved as if in a waking dream, from the room into the hall, to the lift tube, down to the Alien Sector.

Donning a methane breathing apparatus, she made her way to Kosh's quarters, oblivious to the occasional mayhem around her, the fights in the hallways, an unconscious alien with its own protective breathing gear askew on its blue face.

Open the door. Come in.

A final time she sought to flee, but found herself unable to. If she went back to her room now she would never leave it again, but descend into her own mind, into a place of madness from which she would never escape.

The door opened, letting out a fog of methane which brushed over her faceplate.

She went in, and the door closed behind her.

Kosh was there, rising out of the cloud to stand before her.

She asked, "What is it you know? What have you seen?"

Here . . .

Kosh's thoughts opened momentarily to her, in a floodlike light.

"Ohhhh!" she cried, as she was overcome by what washed over her.

And then she was in a place where there were not even dreams . . .

CHAPTER 22

OUT of all the undesirable tasks Commander Susan Ivanova had been asked to perform on Babylon 5, this was by far the most undesirable.

"Can't this wait for Garibaldi?" she begged.

"No, it can't," came Captain Sheridan's voice through her link. "Garibaldi's got his hands full elsewhere. The Life in Transition convention is causing a lot of trouble again; they've gotten out of their auditorium and have started another riot. I'm sorry, Commander, but you'll just have to handle this one yourself. And didn't you tell me you knew something about this Consortium of Live Eaters?"

"Only what I've read," Ivanova said with distaste. "And what I read wasn't pretty."

"Do the best you can. You know they'll only let

one nonspecies authority figure down there. And Commander," the captain added, "be careful."

"I will, Captain."

When the captain had signed off, Ivanova added, "Yech."

Commander Ivanova had never donned an environment suit built to withstand sulphuric acid before.

It was twice as bulky as the standard issue; each joint was double sealed with both steel mesh and a semirigid polymer manufactured to withstand the rabid corrosive powers of the atmosphere the Live Eaters needed to breathe.

In all the time she had been on Babylon 5, Ivanova had never ventured into these particular quarters. Neither had anyone else she had ever talked to. The Live Eaters had become a sort of myth, like the guy with an ax who appears at a camp out, or the headless woman pilot who comes to life at the site of her Starfury accident once a year in Bay 8 on the date it occurred.

But these quarters in the Alien sector were real enough. The Live Eaters had paid for them, credits up front, and had had all the specifications planned down to the tiniest detail. That was the only way they would have been allowed on Babylon 5 in the first place—since the atmosphere they breathed could have burned a hole in the ship otherwise.

But here was Ivanova, standing outside the mythical door, with a suit so heavy it made her feel like she was standing inside Jupiter.

"Here goes nothing," she muttered, and opened the lock that would let her in.

When the lock closed behind her, the small chamber immediately began to fill with sickly yellow fog.

"Yech," Ivanova said again. Out of curiosity, she had brought a writing instrument with her. She now held it out and watched it fizz into mush in her hand.

The inner door of the lock opened, and she was let into the sanctum of the Consortium of Live Eaters.

"Anybody home?" she asked.

"Come in, Commander!" came a cheery voice in her headset.

She stepped into a round room, clear to sight. The atmosphere, thinner than she would have thought, floated at a height of about five feet, thickening toward the ceiling.

A circle of beings, resembling nothing so much as Earth squid, sat, or squatted, or whatever, on the floor, except for the single one whose goggle eyes now stared into her faceplate as his tentacles waggled before him excitedly.

"We are honored that you visit us, Commander! Our humble group, a humble member of the League of Non-Aligned Worlds, is not used to such honor!"

Behind her faceplate, Ivanova gave a slight, uncertain smile. "You're . . . welcome."

One of the alien's tentacles stopped waggling

long enough to point to its red leathery chest. "I am Bish. Again I welcome you."

Bish made an awkward bow, which Ivanova, in her suit, returned just as awkwardly.

"Pleased to meet you, Bish."

Under Bish's huge eyes, his slit of a mouth said, "And to what do we ascribe this honor?"

Ivanova said, "Actually . . . there were reports that you . . . kidnapped someone not of your . . . world?"

"Naturally!" Bish said, in an almost jolly tone. "How else could he partake in our joy!"

Bish pointed with one of his tentacles, and now Ivanova saw, in a corner of the room, a coffin-sized box with a faceplate at one end, through which stared an extremely frightened-looking Centauri.

Commander Ivanova, overcoming her surprise, said, "Umm, may I ask how you got him in here?"

"Of course!" Bish laughed. "We merely asked him to enter the lock and look at the device he now inhabits. He was told there were priceless objects within. Then it was locked, by remote control! Ingenious, don't you think?"

Like catching a mouse with cheese, Ivanova thought. To Bish she said, "Uh, yes. But unfortunately, it's illegal, too. You can't go around kidnapping other inhabitants of Babylon 5. Look in your contract if you don't believe me."

"Nonsense!" Bish chuckled. "Of course we consulted our contract before embarking on this wonderful adventure! And it clearly states, in Paragraph

112, Clause 15a, that others may be solicited to help us with our rites!"

"Solicited doesn't mean kidnapped."

"Of course not! The Centauri was clearly solicited! We asked him if he wanted to enter the box, and he eagerly replied in the affirmative!"

"Well, I have to disagree."

"Very well, Commander. I will not argue with you! It is merely a formality for our Feast and Dissolution Ceremony that we involve an outsider. It need not be the Centauri. Perhaps *you* would like to participate?"

This was said with such good humor that for a moment Commander Ivanova was speechless.

"Ummm—no thank you?"

"Ha ha! As you wish! You realize, of course, that the Feast and Dissolution Ceremony is only enacted during times such as these—when the thought of other races becomes too unbearable to us?"

"I've . . . read something like that," Ivanova said.

Bish laughed. "I only thought that you might feel the same horror and resentment we Live Eaters feel at the moment toward species other than our own! I hope you understand I was trying to be kind, Commander!"

"Uh, yes. And thank you," Ivanova said. "But must you go through with this ceremony? The Worm will be here in a few hours, and after that the crisis will be over, one way or the other."

"No, I'm afraid we can bear this no longer," Bish said cheerfully. "The ceremony will bring us peace." He turned to the circle of sitting Live Eaters and said, "Proceed! And, unfortunately, without an outside guest!"

Immediately, the circle of Live Eaters began to stuff their own mouths with their own tentacles, munching away as if they were eating sandwiches. At the same time, the leathery skin on their hides began to peel away, letting the deadly sulphuric acid of the atmosphere begin to eat away at the flesh within.

Bish, who eagerly joined the circle, called up to Ivanova before putting two of his own tentacles into his mouth, "Good-bye, Commander! And thank you for coming!"

He, too began to both consume himself and be consumed by the acidic atmosphere.

Soon, the circle of Live Eaters had been reduced to bubbling masses of piled organs and hissing skin layers.

To Ivanova, this whole situation with the Worm had just transformed from an external threat to an internal one. The sight did something to her, inside. As much as the nightmares had frightened and angered her, they had not touched her like this, deeply, profoundly. She couldn't take her eyes off them.

CHAPTER 23

On the screen in Captain Sheridan's Command Office, Hilton Dowd looked very unhappy.

"I can't emphasize enough how displeased President Clark is with your response to your present threat," the man said. He looked as if he, too, had had little sleep recently—though the Worm undoubtedly was not the cause of it, in his case.

"President Clark should understand that we've done everything possible to keep order on Babylon 5 *and* to try to understand what we're up against. And I prefer not to call the Worm a threat; it has evidenced no overt hostility toward Babylon 5. The only threat has been the nightmares, whose connection to the Worm remains unclear."

"Oh? I hope you're not as ignorant as you sound."

Taking a deep breath, Sheridan ignored the insult. "Prudent action is the course, at the moment."

"We are beginning to think otherwise. All travel to Babylon 5 has been suspended for the time being, and we are considering closing the Epsilon jump gate to all traffic, and banning all jumps in the vicinity of Babylon 5 for the foreseeable future."

"That would cause havoc here! I have near panic here as it is! If you ban all jumps in this area, it will just send a message to the inhabitants of this station that Earth Central thinks they're doomed! There'll be real panic then!"

"I said we are considering that option. We are also considering an all-out attack on the Worm."

"A military assault! Have you lost your mind!"

On the screen, Dowd's tired eyes grew suddenly steely and hard. "I would like to remind you, Captain, that when you address me you might as well be addressing President Clark himself."

Again, Sheridan drew a deep breath. "I only meant to point out," he said, reasonably, "that we have no reason to assault the Worm at this time."

"You may receive orders to do so in the future."

"Before that option is even seriously considered, I'd like to send a manned scientific expedition to the Worm. It is something we've already been considering."

"I know."

Again, Sheridan was made aware that Earth

Central had been getting information from Babylon 5 illicitly; but he chose to say nothing.

"Then we'll proceed with the scientific expedition."

"That's the only constructive thing you have done, Captain. We need that data."

Before Sheridan could say anything further, the screen went blank.

"Damn," the captain muttered in frustration.

An hour later, Commander Ivanova had assembled her scientific team in front of Shuttle 2.

It was a small group, consisting of Ivanova herself, three techs named Armstrong, Povin, and Mitchell, a shuttle pilot named Anders, and Dr. Creighton Laramie, of Barker Industries, an Earth concern. Laramie had recommended himself to Ivanova as an expert in plasma physics, and had been working furiously to try to extract whatever secrets he could from the Worm.

"So far," he said laconically, "I've been able to learn this much about the Worm." He curled the thumb and forefinger of his right hand into a zero. He was a tall, thin, and nearly bald man with no laugh lines on his face. "Perhaps when we're closer . . ."

"Well, I hope we can find something out, Doctor," Ivanova said. She turned to Armstrong, the short, overeager head of the tech group. "Are you ready?"

"Ready as we'll ever be. The shuttle's been outfitted and is ready to go. We'll be up close and personal with the Worm in no time." There was almost pleasure in the tech's eyes, which made Ivanova pause for a second.

"Armstrong, are you all right?"

"Just tired," Armstrong said. He laughed shortly. "Just bad dreams, like everybody else."

After a moment's hesitation, Ivanova said, "All right." She turned to Creighton Laramie. "Are you ready, Doctor?"

Laramie nodded, unsmiling. "Yes." Without another word he turned and boarded the shuttle.

Commander Ivanova, taking a deep breath, said, "Let's go then," and followed.

Ivanova and the others felt a nice kick pushing them back into their seats as the shuttle's thrusters neutralized Babylon 5's imparted rotational force. Almost immediately, they were on line to the Worm, which grew by the minute in the shuttle's forward windows.

Dr. Laramie spent no time looking at the Worm; as soon as he had Ivanova's all-clear he was out of his seat and in the back of the ship, attending to his own instrumentation. Ivanova wandered back after a few moments and found Laramie hovering over a very elaborate system of scanners, of remarkably compact design.

"Your company produced this equipment, Doctor?" she asked, pleasantly.

Curtly, Laramie replied, "With help, yes."

"It's very advanced."

This time, Laramie only scowled, leaving Ivanova

to wander back up front and sit beside the pilot, Anders. Through the windows, the green ribbon of the Worm grew brighter by the minute. They seemed to be heading straight for one of the twists, the curl of which began to nearly fill the screen.

"Have a nice chat with the mad scientist, Commander?" Anders joked.

"Not really," Ivanova said. "He seems a little lost in his equipment."

"Well, maybe he'll be able to tell you something."

"I hope so," Ivanova said, furrowing her brow in thought. "I hope so."

The Worm seemed to engulf them. The rest of space had been nearly subsumed by the glowing band.

"It's much brighter up close," Ivanova said.

Behind her, just emerging from his equipment bay, Dr. Laramie said, "Actually, it has no brightness at all. What you are looking at is an illusion of brightness."

Ivanova looked back at the doctor. "I don't understand."

"The Worm does not exist; at least, not in our universe. We do not have one recording that tells us that it physically exists. What we have been able to measure is a . . . phantom. The particles that make it up are not real particles, but ghosts of particles."

"Ghosts? Ghosts of what?"

But already Laramie had ducked back into his equipment bay, closing the door behind him.

The shuttle cruised along the edge of the Worm.

It was like running a dune cycle along the beach. The Worm curled and flattened like waves as they passed close along its edge: hills turned abruptly into valleys, valleys into hills.

"It's actually rather beautiful," Commander Ivanova said.

"But nonexistent," Anders said.

"That's correct," Laramie agreed. They turned to look at him. "I've taken scans and photographs, and not one has showed anything other than nothingness. I would appreciate it if you begin our pass through the Worm now."

"I'll contact Captain Sheridan," Ivanova said.

But once again Laramie had disappeared into his sanctum, closing the door behind him.

On the communication screen in front of her, Captain Sheridan looked worried.

"I still don't like the idea of you going through that thing," he said.

Ivanova said, "Captain, we both know that it's the only way to find out what effect it will have on B5 when the station passes through it. And that's only twenty hours away."

"I know. But it makes me feel like I've turned you into a guinea pig. I should have gone myself."

"You put me in charge of the science team. And you're needed on the station."

"Still . . ."

"Do I have your permission to pass through the Worm, Captain?"

Ivanova could sense Sheridan's sense of duty overwhelming his concern.

"Permission granted, Commander. But proceed cautiously—and back out immediately if you sense danger to yourself or the shuttle."

"Thank you, Captain," Ivanova said.

"No—thank *you,* Commander," Sheridan said, signing off.

"Prepare for passage through the Worm—" Ivanova began to announce, but suddenly there was a commotion behind her.

The science tech Armstrong had appeared, wild-eyed, waving a large spanner like a club.

"You can't do this!" he shouted. "You can't go through that thing!"

Behind him, another of the techs, Mitchell, appeared.

"Commander!" he said, staying clear of Armstrong, who brandished his weapon at the man. "Armstrong hurt Povin, bad! If we don't get him back to B5 I think we'll lose him!"

Ivanova slowly got out of her couch and approached Armstrong with her hand out.

"Give me the spanner," she said evenly.

Armstrong grunted loudly and swung the weapon at Ivanova. Ivanova evaded the swing, stepped quickly forward, and kicked him in the side. The spanner clattered to the floor as the tech fell forward.

Ivanova kicked Armstrong again when he tried to rise, then put her knee into his back while Mitchell fetched a length of electrical cable. Ivanova hog-tied Armstrong's hands and feet. "Stay still, before you cause any more damage." The enormity of the crisis finally hit her. If they couldn't control themselves, they had no chance against the Worm.

She rose and followed Mitchell to where Povin lay in a heap against a storage locker; the deep gash in the back of his head was all the evidence Ivanova needed in order to know the extent of his injury. With less than twenty hours until the Worm reached B5, she was going to have to abort the mission. The thought made her sick, but she had no choice.

Mitchell said, "He tried to tell Armstrong that it would be fine when we went through the Worm, but he just went nuts! I think he's been having dreams about being smothered by a Narn, and he thought the Worm would smother us."

"Anders!" Ivanova shouted up front. "Turn us around and head home! Flank speed!"

Dr. Creighton Laramie appeared. Two spots of anger colored his cheeks. "Do you mean to say we're not going to pass through the Worm?" he asked.

"If we don't get this man back to B5 immediately, he'll die. And I won't let that happen."

Laramie moved closer, accentuating his height advantage. "But we may not get another chance to do this!"

"The discussion is over, Doctor," Commander Ivanova said. "We're going back to Babylon 5."

CHAPTER 24

SHERIDAN and Garibaldi were waiting for Ivanova in the docking bay. After Dr. Laramie had brushed angrily past, and Povin had been rushed to Medlab, the captain turned to Ivanova and said, "All hell has broken loose. That Life in Transition group is barricaded in their conference room, and the Fermi's Angels are trying to knock down the door to get to them. Three bikers are already in Medlab. Also, the Centauri and Narn have decided to fight a little war of their own on Babylon 5, and have been shooting at each other in the vicinity of the Zocolo.

"Commander, I want you to handle the bikers. And Garibaldi, I want you to get on the Centauri situation. Report back to me every fifteen minutes."

Garibaldi said to Ivanova, "Tell Carbon, the leader of the Angels, that if he's a good boy I'll show him pictures of my Ninja ZX-11 cycle."

"I'll tell him that—after I finish breaking his head," Ivanova said.

The open air market of the Zocolo was nearly deserted. But Garibaldi could hear the sound of random shooting as he approached.

The area was half destroyed, with litter and broken furniture everywhere. Some of the lights had been shot out.

"Security personal in the vicinity of the Zocolo, check in," Garibaldi said into his link.

There was silence for a moment, and then a lone voice, sounding scared, said, "Templeton here, sir."

"Templeton—are you the only one?"

"Yes, sir. I called for backup, but none's available."

"Where are you?"

"Behind the bar, sir. I've been pinned down for about an hour."

A shot came somewhere in front of Garibaldi, followed by an answering shot from somewhere else.

"How many of them are there?"

"Four, I think. Two Narns and two Centauri. There were a lot more before all the damage was done. They carted a few away, and then most of the fighting moved off."

"Stay where you are," Garibaldi said, trying not

to sound as mad as he was. "I'll be back in a little while with help."

"Oh, and sir?"

"What is it, Templeton?"

"There's someone else with me behind the bar, here. It's Ambassador Mollari."

"Put him on."

"I can't do that, sir."

"He's not hurt, is he?"

There came a pause.

"Templeton—answer me!"

"The ambassador's not hurt, sir. He's dead drunk."

Sighing with relief, Garibaldi said, "Stay there with him. I'll be back soon."

Tracking G'Kar down proved more difficult than Garibaldi had thought it would. Finally, after trying a couple of possible haunts, the security chief retreated to Security Central, where, to his astonishment, he found only one ensign present—and she was asleep at her console, moaning with bad dreams.

Shaking the ensign awake, Garibaldi said, "O'Connor—snap out of it!"

O'Connor came suddenly awake and looked up into Garibaldi's face with horror.

"Minbari, sir! Hateful! Hate—"

Garibaldi gave her a firm slap across the face, and she began to weep.

"I'm . . . sorry, Chief. It's just that, when I sleep, I dream, and the dreams are so *horrible.*"

"It's all right. Why are you alone?"

Coming under a measure of control, the ensign said, "The rest . . . couldn't handle it. There were fights and shouting. I sent them all off duty. I thought I could handle it by myself . . ."

Garibaldi helped her from her chair.

"You did a hell of a job, O'Connor." He fished in his pocket for one of Dr. Franklin's horse pills, which he pressed into her hand. "Now take this, and get some real sleep. I'll see you in about four hours."

O'Connor nodded and stumbled off, leaving Garibaldi alone in Security Central.

Quickly he checked the various views, not liking what he was seeing. Everywhere, there seemed to be chaos. Most of it was spiraling out of the control of his forces—none of which looked well rested. He would have to get more of Franklin's magic pills for his officers. It was the only way to hold things together.

He was about to send out an all-points bulletin for G'Kar, when, as if by magic, the Narn appeared in his doorway.

"I thought you might want to consult with me," G'Kar said formally.

"Boy, do I! Come with me!"

And nearly yanking G'Kar by the hand, Garibaldi headed back toward the Zocolo.

CHAPTER 25

When Commander Ivanova arrived at the Life in Transition conference room, there wasn't much conference room left.

The doors had long since been blasted away by the repeated blows of plasma cycles fitted with crash fronts that resembled battering rams.

The LITs had erected barricades, but these were in the process of being pulled apart by other cycles with chains afixed to the barriers. A hooting biker roared past Ivanova as she arrived, bearing the trophy of a piece of a Life in Transition member's suit; it was a chunk of mica, which the biker threw against the nearest wall.

Ivanova drew her weapon and approached a

group of bikers who stood astride their parked vehicles, conversing.

"Any of you Carbon?" Ivanova asked.

Carbon emerged from the group and, ignoring Ivanova's weapon, said angrily, "Yeah. And who are you?"

"Commander Ivanova, Executive Officer of Babylon 5."

Carbon stood with massive arms folded, scowling. "So what do *you* want?"

"So I'd like you to get your group to disperse." Ivanova looked around her, searching for security personnel.

"If you're looking for the fuzz, we scattered them a long time ago," Carbon said. Behind him in the biker group there were titters.

Into her link, Ivanova said, "Security Central, this is Ivanova. I need backup at Conference Room 3."

She waited, but there was no answer. "Security Central," she repeated.

Nothing.

Ivanova returned her attention to the still-tittering bikers. "As I said, I'd like you to disperse!"

"Like I told the cops before I chased 'em off, I'm gonna tell you: those Lite-heads in there have blasphemed! They've put out a proclamation that the Worm that's appeared outside this station is not a sign from God that life exists everywhere, but that it's proof that life shouldn't exist anywhere! Can you believe that?"

"Actually, what I believe doesn't mean anything

at the moment; what does is that you're destroying Babylon 5 property and threatening the well-being of another guest group on this station."

Carbon scowled at Ivanova, then suddenly burst into a laugh. "You hear that, people?" he shouted. "The little gal here says we've got to disperse!"

There was raucous laughter, and Silicon emerged from the crowd, holding a pipe in her hand. She brought her face up close to Commander Ivanova's and smiled. She said, "Let's show the little lady here just how fast we can disperse!"

Behind Silicon, one of the Angels mounted his hog and kick-started it into life. With a roar he skidded away from the conference room wall, sped back twenty yards, then skidded around and headed at top speed straight for the opening where the doorway had been. Hitting a slight ramp, he tore off through the opening with a whoop and disappeared inside.

In a moment, fresh howls broke out within the conference room, and now another and then another of the Angels followed the first one, diving through the opening on their roaring machines.

Silicon kept her smile on Ivanova. "Like what you see, sweetie?"

The commander raised her link and said, "Garibaldi! Come in!"

"You know the chief?" Carbon said, immediately interested.

"Of course," Ivanova said. Into the link she implored, "Garibaldi!"

"What is it?" Garibaldi said, sounding harried himself.

"I need your assistance!" Ivanova said.

"Uh . . . can't get to you at the moment. I'm sort of pinned down with G'Kar. We're on our way to bigger problems."

In the background, Commander Ivanova heard the sound of PPG shots.

"Is that the chief?" Carbon said. "Let me talk to 'im, man!"

"Uh . . ." Ivanova said, but Carbon had already grabbed her wrist and was talking into the link.

"Chief! How's it goin' man!"

"Uh . . . Carbon?"

"You bet, dude!"

There was a pause while shots were fired in the background.

"Um, what are you up to, Carbon? Not giving my main squeeze Susan a hard time, are you?"

"She's your back rider, man? Jeez, I'm sorry! I didn't know!"

"It's okay, Carbon. But cut her some slack, okay?"

"Whatever you say, man!"

Again there was gunfire in the background.

Carbon said, "Hey, you're not in trouble, are you, dude?"

Garibaldi said, "Uh, sort of."

"Well then, we'll bail you out, man!"

"That would be . . . just fine, Carbon. I'm . . . sort of in the Zocolo."

Carbon turned around to the Angels and

shouted, "Hey! Listen up! We've got some work to do! Haul it out—now!"

Instantly, the cycles began to leave the conference room, roaring out and lining up. Carbon turned to Susan and said, "I'm truly sorry for the bad behavior, ma'am. Truly sorry."

Somewhat dazed, Ivanova stood back while the Fermi's Angels roared off in the direction of the Zocolo. She noted the sour look that Silicon gave her as she sped past.

"Chief could'a done better with me," Silicon said, in a huff.

In a moment Commander Ivanova was left alone, watching a trail of settling dust. Slowly, she picked her way through the wreckage to the opening in the conference room.

Inside was a shambles, with holes in all the walls and in the ceiling. On the floor lay a moaning mass of Life in Transition conferees, holding their heads and various other limbs. Pieces of their mineral suits were scattered here and there.

She looked down at them, a deep exhaustion filling her. "You guys might have a point about life being a mistake," she mumbled under her breath, before bending down to help one up.

CHAPTER 26

GARIBALDI wasn't sure that even a bunch of bikers could help him now.

He never thought he'd be in this position on B5, hiding with the Narn ambassador behind a food cart and praying for his life. When he'd tried to contact security officer Templeton again, he'd found her unresponsive; as he and G'Kar had gotten closer to the Zocolo they discovered that the fight had returned, and there was Templeton, unconscious, on the floor near the bar she had been hiding behind.

Leaving G'Kar safely behind, he'd been able to make his way to the bar—but then discovered to his horror that the Centauri ambassador, Londo Mollari, was gone.

"We have him!" came a cry, from far off at the other end of the market.

G'Kar called out, "Who dares to do this thing!"

"We have listened to you for far too long, and now is the time for Narn justice!" came the reply.

G'Kar ordered, "Release Ambassador Mollari immediately!"

"He will be tried, as the Centauri criminal he is!"

Shots were fired, pinning Garibaldi where he was.

"At least let me attend to my officer!" Garibaldi shouted, his eyes on Templeton, who did not look good.

"Do what you want—when we are gone!"

Then there followed a bevy of shots.

Suddenly, the other end of the market erupted in the sounds of Fermi's Angels tearing in, knocking aside whatever chairs and tables had thus far been spared.

"Garibaldi, my man, we have arrived!" Carbon shouted.

The Narn combatants fled, their guns going silent. Garibaldi stood up slowly. Now the Zocolo was quiet, save for the purring of plasma motorcycle engines.

Carbon kickstanded his bike and strode over to the Security Chief, slapping him hard on the back.

"Glad to be of service, man!"

"Can you help me with my officer?"

"Sure thing, man!" Carbon said, lifting Templeton up as if she were a rag doll. Garibaldi was happy to hear her let out a soft moan.

"Where you want her, man?"

"Medlab," Garibaldi said.

"Sure thing. Medlab, people!" Carbon ordered, and in a moment the cycles were gone in the same whirlwind in which they had arrived, leaving Garibaldi to approach G'Kar.

"We've got big problems now," Garibaldi said.

"Yes," G'Kar said, "we do."

In twenty minutes, Chief Garibaldi had gathered every available security officer, which wasn't as many as he needed. He knew that Centauri gangs were already patrolling Babylon 5 in search of Londo; his only hope was that he would find the ambassador before anyone else did.

G'Kar professed not to know who had kidnapped Mollari. "They are most likely refugees," he said. "None of those whom I know personally are involved, so far as I can tell. I must confess to dreaming about this very occurrence, and in my dream it led to an all-out war on Babylon 5. A horrible, disturbing dream."

"And that's why you'll help me find Londo, right?" Garibaldi asked.

The Narn made a sour face before stating, "Though I personally hope he dies a thousand painful deaths, I will help you for that reason. And for that reason alone."

"Good." The security chief made a sour face of his own. "Now all we need is a lot of luck."

* * *

They began their search in the Narn quarters, but it quickly became apparent that Ambassador Mollari would not be found there. Extensive damage had already occurred due to Centauri attacks, and the Narn were obviously hiding Mollari elsewhere.

"I'm afraid," G'Kar said solemnly, "that this search could go on for weeks, with no success. I don't want this to sound like bragging, Mr. Garibaldi, but my people can be very resourceful when they want to be."

Garibaldi was about to answer when his link sounded.

"Garibaldi here."

"Chief?" came a call from Security Central. "We've had a message from Ambassador Mollari's kidnappers. They say that if you don't call off your search immediately they'll kill him. They say they have him in a place you can't get to easily, and that they'll know if you're coming. They sound like they mean it, Chief. We weren't able to lock in on where the communication came from, though I doubt they made it from the same spot they're keeping the ambassador in."

"That's for sure."

"They say they'll call back in ten minutes, and they want an answer. And they said they'll know if you're complying or not."

Garibaldi considered for a moment.

"What shall I tell them, Chief?"

"Tell them it's a deal. But tell them that if they hurt the ambassador in any way, everything is over for them. Got that?"

"Got it, Chief."

"And try again to lock onto that call—it might give us a clue to where they're hiding him."

"Right."

Garibaldi signed off, and turned to face G'Kar.

G'Kar asked, "Will you really do what you say?"

"I have no choice, G'Kar. The way tensions are running now, I've got to believe they'll kill Mollari if we get too close."

G'Kar nodded. "I'm afraid I must concur. I know my people, and I believe they would do what they say."

"The thing is, what will they do with Londo now?"

Ten minutes later, Garibaldi's link chimed again.

"Garibaldi here."

"Chief? We've heard from the kidnappers again. They say it's good that you have done what they've demanded. They say they know where you are now, and that if you had continued to search, then Ambassador Mollari would be dead by now. They say we'd better continue to stay away."

"Were you able to trace the transmission?"

"Yes, a scan took us to a service elevator not fifty feet from where you are now, Chief."

"I'm sure the elevator is empty now."

"That's not all, Chief. They said that Ambassador Mollari will now be put on trial, and that if he is found guilty of the crimes he has committed, he will be put to death."

CHAPTER 27

MINBARI Ambassador Delenn slept—but now it was not a pleasant sleep.

The last time she had slept, in the briefing room with Captain Sheridan's coat draped over her, she had slept deeply and awakened refreshed. The dreams had been there, but they had been pushed to the side, made secondary. They had been curiosities she had observed, not dramas she had participated in.

But now she was a participant again—and once again, Captain John Sheridan was her foe.

They were in a huge amphitheater, under the bluest of skies dotted with the faintest of clouds. The field of the amphitheater was of green grass, evenly cut and unmarked from wall to wall. In the stands was a packed throng of people—though when Delenn looked up to see them she could not make out their faces. Either there was sun in her eyes, or shadows fell across the stands—but the spectators were a faceless throng of cheering beings.

And then the cheers rose.

She looked far across the field, and saw John Sheridan riding toward her on a strange, six-legged animal which resembled an Earth horse. Its head was thrown back in the passion of the ride, as its legs clumped like pistons on the turf, throwing up clods of dirt and grass behind it. On its face was a mixture of terror and hatred; its nostrils were flared and steaming breath, its lips pulled back over huge white teeth, which were slightly parted to show a bloodred tongue within, around which foam frothed. Its eyes were wide, the pupils hard as black stones.

John Sheridan, on the animal's back, looked no less angry.

He was dressed for battle, in metal-jointed clothing of bright colors: on the breast of his chain-mail shirt was a huge blue representation of the planet Earth. His hands were gloved in thick black leather; on his head was a battle helmet, the visor thrown back to show his fierce features.

Borne tightly in the crook of his arm was a long silver spear, ended with the sharpest blade Delenn had ever seen.

"Delenn!" he shouted, arched forward in his saddle, eager for battle. "Prepare to die!"

Suddenly Delenn found herself on her own six-legged mount, hurtling toward Captain Sheridan. She wore chain mail similar to his own, only on her own breast was depicted Minbari in all its splendor.

She bore her own lance, its tip no less sharp than that of the captain's.

The roar of the horses' hoofs as they pounded the grassy turf became even more deafening than the roars of the crowd in the seats.

The two riders hurtled toward one another. Delenn concentrated on Sheridan's face, which bore nothing but hatred.

The horses flew by one another, and Captain Sheridan's lance barely missed Delenn, as Delenn's own missed him.

The crowd gave a roar of disappointment as the riders rode past one another before stopping and slowly turning to face one another again.

"This time you will die, Delenn!" John Sheridan cried.

Delenn felt fear crawl into her stomach as once again the captain kicked his animal into an angry run.

Reluctantly, Delenn urged her own mount onward, lifting her lance to point at the breast of John Sheridan.

The horses bore down on one another, chests moving like deep bellows, hooves pushing into the ground, pounding forward—

John Sheridan looked with deep hatred into her eyes as he raised his own lance and held it firm, its point a dagger arrowed at her heart.

The two horses met.

Both lances found their marks.

Delenn and Sheridan were thrown from their beasts to the ground. The lances were ripped from their grips by the blows, yet neither had been pierced. Both had been saved by their armor.

Delenn lay breathless upon the ground for a moment, and then, sensing danger, pushed herself to her feet.

Her mount had stopped nearby and she ran to it, drawing a sword from its scabbard.

Sheridan advanced on her with a battle-ax, murder in his eyes.

"Die now!" he shouted, raising the ax and bringing it down at her.

She raised her sword in defense, warding off the blow, driven to one knee.

Again the ax rose and fell.

"Die!" Sheridan shouted.

Delenn blocked the blow, but was driven down farther toward the ground.

In her ears, the roar of the crowd increased; she glanced over now and saw that the stands were filled with humans, on their feet and cheering.

"Die!" John Sheridan ordered.

Up went the ax; down it drove again, this time knocking the sword from her hand.

"John—please!" she said, holding her hands out before her.

He stepped astride her body and raised the ax yet higher over his head, pausing to let the crowd's cheers reach their peak.

Down it came.

CHAPTER 28

WHERE . . .

Martina Coles awoke, with the humming even louder in her head. She could not concentrate on anything—could not even, for a moment, remember who she was.

Where . . .

In panic, she looked up at a face she knew but did not know; she looked left and right and saw a place she knew but did not recognize.

She tried to move but could not . . .

"What . . . is happening to me?"

"Try to relax," the voice connected to the face she knew but did not know, said. "You're in your own quarters, now. Ambassador Kosh called us and said that you were unconscious. He tried to revive you but was unable. He was afraid that his methane atmosphere would poison you, so he finally called us to come and retrieve you.

Now she knew the face.

Knew . . .

Garibaldi.

"I—"

Garibaldi put his finger to his lips, shushing her. "Don't say anything yet. I've got a pill from Dr. Franklin that will help you get some real sleep. Then we'll talk."

The security chief helped her take the last of his sleeping pills and held a glass of water to her lips while she drank. As he cradled her neck, he could feel the tension that was always in her. He lay her head back down and smiled.

"In a couple of hours, I'll be back."

To his surprise, she nodded and gave a slight smile herself.

"Yes . . ." she said.

"Good," Garibaldi said, getting up and turning out the light as he left.

There it was, in her mind.

The buzzing was gone in the back of her head: the pill had reduced it to a gentle, almost soothing hum. And there was nothing else in her mind but the Worm.

It floated before her, turning like a ribbon, seeming to dance for her. As she reached out to take hold of it, to perhaps ride it like a dolphin through space, it gently twisted away from her touch. Again she reached out to it, her fingers trying to take hold, and it seemed to sense her and pull back in avoidance.

And yet she moved above it, around it, over it, and it stretched vast and wide and green and shimmering.

And now when she darted her hand forward, it went into the Worm; into nothing at all . . .

In three hours Garibaldi was back, along with a harried Captain Sheridan. One sleeve of Garibaldi's jacket was ripped and as she sat up in bed Martina stared at it.

Garibaldi grinned tiredly. "Got into a little scuffle with a couple of Drazi a half hour ago. They got the sleeve but I got the collar."

Captain Sheridan said, "Ms. Coles, I'm going to ask you to tell us what you know about the Worm."

Martina said, "I know nothing about it."

Sheridan looked annoyed, and Garibaldi quickly stepped forward.

"Just tell us what happened when you talked to Kosh," he said.

Martina said, "Kosh . . . opened something up to me. Gave me a glance of something he himself saw. He was . . . greatly troubled by it, or . . ." She looked up at Garibaldi. "I would have to say he was shocked."

Captain Sheridan said, "What did it feel like? Give us . . . any impressions you had of why the Worm is here."

"I have no idea why the Worm is here. All I can tell you is the impression I get of it."

"Which is . . . ?"

"It's . . . like a ghost of something."

Not able to hide his frustration, Captain Sheridan said, "That doesn't *tell* me anything!"

Martina looked at him evenly. "That's all I know."

"Is it going to harm us? Is it here to destroy us? *These* are the things I need to know to make decisions!"

"I can only tell you what I know."

"I have to talk to Kosh," Sheridan said. "And I want you to try to read him again."

"He won't let me," Martina said, firmly. Already she felt the buzz beginning to build in the back of her head once more, as the pill wore off. "And I'm afraid I won't be of much use to you from now on."

"Why?" Garibaldi said.

"Because the Worm is too strong in my head. It's . . . overwhelming me."

"Perhaps Dr. Franklin can help," Garibaldi said, as Martina lay back with her eyes closed. The buzz was becoming a roar, now.

"God, it's getting closer . . ." Martina moaned.

"It will pass through Babylon 5 in twelve hours," Captain Sheridan said. "Are you sure, Ms. Coles, that there's nothing you can tell us about its intentions?"

"I can tell you this," Martina said, her eyes

tightly closed against the pain. "From what I read, I sensed no intentions at all from the Worm. Nothing. Which means that anything could happen when we pass through it." She grimaced in pain. "Anything."

CHAPTER 29

THERE were three unconscious bodies in the Alien Sector, which Sheridan had to deal with before he reached Kosh's quarters. Everything was falling apart.

The door to Kosh's quarters opened, and he entered.

There was a swirl of methane as the door closed behind Sheridan, and then the Vorlon ambassador came forward out of a cloud to greet them.

Kosh's speaking device irised open.

"Captain," the Vorlon said simply.

Sheridan said respectfully, "Ambassador, I'm here to ask you a great favor. We've talked with the Psi Corps representative, Martina Coles, who said that she had an audience with you in which you let her read you."

After a moment, the speaker irised, giving a tinkling mixture of music and words. "That is not quite true."

"Perhaps you could elaborate?" Captain Sheridan said.

The Vorlon was silent.

"Ambassador," Sheridan said, "did you let Ms. Coles read you or not?"

"She saw . . . a fragment."

"So you did let her read you?"

"As I said: a fragment . . ."

"And what was that fragment? A portion of the nature of the Worm?"

The Vorlon was silent.

"Look," Captain Sheridan said, "I hope you realize the position I'm in, Ambassador. The Worm is twelve hours away, and I know practically nothing about it. Earth Central is pressuring me to attack it, while at the same time the nightmares are literally tearing my ship apart from within. I *have* to know everything I can about it. Now, have or have you not garnered any information about the Worm?"

After a moment, the Vorlon said, "I have studied it."

"And what can you tell me?"

"I can tell you nothing."

Trying not to grow angry, Sheridan said, "What does that mean?"

The Vorlon moved incrementally back away

from Sheridan, and the captain suddenly realized that Kosh did not want him there.

"Ambassador, does it bother you that I'm here?"

"It is difficult to be with others at the moment."

"So it's affecting you, too? The same thing that has affected the rest of the station?"

"Yes."

Deciding to try again, Sheridan said, "I will leave as soon as I can, Ambassador. But I must ask you again: what have you learned in your study of the Worm?"

"I have learned . . . nothing."

"Nothing?"

"What I gave Ms. Coles was all that she could stand to see. A portion of . . . nothing."

"You're speaking in riddles, Ambassador," Sheridan said with irritation. "I thought we were moving beyond that stage."

"I tell you what I know."

"Is there anything you can tell me to help me save Babylon 5? Anything at all?"

The ambassador moved farther back; now the Vorlon was partially engulfed in swirling methane fog.

Kosh's speaking device opened; but only a tinkle of faraway sounding music came out.

"Ambassador?" Captain Sheridan asked.

"Please . . . go . . ." the Vorlon said, moving back into the cloud of methane until he could no longer be seen.

* * *

After the human had left, Kosh was given over to the swirl of his alien mind.

In it, a great storm raged, and in the middle of the storm, in a place that was like dreams, twisted a monstrous green shape, long like a snake that filled the skies, and that blazed in the Vorlon's thoughts like a million bright suns, burning.

CHAPTER 30

"YOU can't leave!" Commander Ivanova ordered. She stood her ground, but against the mob that was forming in front of her, she didn't know how long she could hold out.

Into her link she said, for the third time, "This is Commander Ivanova; please send a security team to Cargo Bay 8! This is an emergency request!"

And again, the link gave her a hiss of unanswered noise in return. Which meant that Security Central was unmanned, or worse.

Standing between the freighter *Pegasus,* which was still nestled tight in its bay, thrusters toward the bay's huge outer door, and the growing mob of passengers who wanted to board it, Ivanova felt very much alone. She knew that her success in this situation depended entirely on her ability to deal with the captain of the vessel.

She turned her weapon on the bearded man who stood beside her, and made sure everyone knew the PPG was ready to fire at maximum.

"Captain Hendricks?" Commander Ivanova said to the man, who looked as startled as his passengers.

"What is it, Commander?" Hendricks said.

"I'm going to give you a simple choice. Either you disperse your passengers, who you have charged outrageous prices to leave Babylon 5 packed like cattle on your cargo freighter, or I will shoot you. I have the authority, and I will use it. You have attempted to leave Babylon 5 without my authorization as traffic controller, and have caused me to leave my post in the Observation Dome to come down here and personally stop you. If you leave now, overcrowded and overweight, there is a good chance that you will injure or kill all of these people whom you have fleeced. Your passengers should be aware of the fact that even if you successfully leave Babylon 5 without getting fired on by any of the various fighters, Narn, Minbari, Earth, or Centauri or otherwise that are now in the vicinity, your whereabouts will be tracked and you will be brought to justice later. The only way you get out of this intact and unprosecuted is if you tell these people to leave now and lock down your ship until further notice."

For a moment there was utter silence, as Commander Ivanova's hand held the PPG in a tight grip aimed at Hendricks, but then someone in the crowd said, "Nice speech—but how do we get off B5 if we want to?"

"There's no reason to leave Babylon 5," Ivanova said. "There's no reason to believe that the Worm has any hostile intentions toward us."

There was an outcry from the crowd, as various voices made their feelings heard:

"Babylon 5 won't exist in eight hours!"

"The Worm will destroy us!"

"I don't want to die!"

"Let us leave now!"

"The Minbari will kill us all!"

"I hate the Narn!"

"Let us go!"

Commander Ivanova shouted, "Please listen—"

But suddenly she was jostled as the mob surged forward, and then she was knocked to the ground, the weapon knocked from her grasp. As people stumbled past her, she crawled quickly to the side and turned to watch as Captain Hendricks was also pushed aside in a general rush to his ship.

My God, Commander Ivanova thought, *they'll tear this bay to pieces.*

She stood and shouted, "Stop!" but it was too late; a mob had rushed for the open hatch, and already a few had been trampled. From within the *Pegasus* came an ominous sound of thrusters being fired up prematurely. Ivanova saw Captain Hendricks desperately trying to claw his way through the crowd. For a moment he looked back at Ivanova, and then he was carried along in the tumult, toward the open hatch.

The freighter's thrusters gave a tentative snort, sending a blast of heat and fire which blackened the bay's sealed door into space.

Suddenly there was a reversal of the mob's tide.

"Get out!" someone shouted. "Get out while you can!"

The *Pegasus*'s thrusters fired again briefly, rocking the freighter in its cradle. One of the bay door's seals, singed by the thrusters second firing, ruptured, and now the deadly vacuum of space began to slowly trade places with the oxygenated bay.

Ivanova shouted into her link, "C and C! We have a hull rupture in Docking Bay 8!"

Pulling at the passenger nearest to her, a wild-eyed woman clutching a small boy to her side, Commander Ivanova pushed to the bay's open interior door.

"Get out!" she said, shoving them through. A startled old man stumbled by and she grabbed at his arm and pushed him through the opening after the other two.

"You too! Come with us!" cried the hysterical woman, letting go of her son to pull Susan off balance through the opening, just as the automatic seals closed it behind her.

Ivanova fought herself to her feet and saw, through the sealed door's window, a scene of horror unfold within Docking Bay 8.

With a rumble, the *Pegasus*'s engines fired a third time, blowing the docking bay's door out into space.

Instantly, the bay's air and pressure were sucked away. The freighter rocked on its cradle and broke away; around it, whatever passengers hadn't made it onto the ship were pulled out into space, seemingly sucked up and away by B5's spin.

Now, as if in a dream, the *Pegasus* was yanked out of the dock. Ivanova could see someone desperately closing the freighter's hatch even as the ship turned and then fired its thrusters.

For a moment it looked as if the freighter might have a chance, but then a shuttle hove into view and hit the *Pegasus* broadside, rupturing its hull.

As Ivanova lost sight of it, the freighter's thrusters were firing in vain bursts, even as the rear of the ship burst into flame.

Ivanova turned to look at the passengers behind her, but they were gone. Already technicians were racing toward her, ready to do what they could to help, which was nothing.

Beyond exhaustion and shock, Ivanova headed for the Observation Dome and whatever new horrors awaited her there.

CHAPTER 31

THE Reverend Bobby James Galaxy was given a dream, and in the dream was the Final Plan.

The leader of the Universal Church of Solar Illumination was used to dreams. Dreams had guided him his entire life. First he had dreamed of selling used vehicles in the city of Baltimore on Earth—stolen vehicles, that is—and then, when things had gotten too hot on Earth, he had moved to the vast open territory of Mars.

Things had gone well there for a while, and his dreams had been good ones: he had dreamed of owning a lot of credits, and the credits had come, since the sale of certain merchandise, among them weapons of every sort, had been a lucrative business on Mars. He had dreamed of women, and he had

had women; he had dreamed of luxury, and he had had luxury.

He hadn't dreamed of Earthforce catching up with him, over a little matter of weapon sales to rebel forces—but had dreamed, long before, of a forged identicard and an escape route if some such unpleasantness should happen: which was how he had found his way to Babylon 5.

And his time on B5 had been . . . lucrative. In Down Below, where all sorts of things were peddled by all sorts of people, Bobby James Galaxy (or, as he had been known in his former days, Harold Schneckelheimer) found a ready audience for what he was now selling, since the coming of the Worm, which was . . . salvation.

Salvation was a valuable product to Lurkers, who had little reason to dream of it themselves. But Bobby James Galaxy had come along and dreamed it for them, and they had responded with an affinity that was astounding.

It was even easier than selling PPGs to people who wanted very much to shoot other people.

But now, strangely . . . the dreams had turned more urgent. Where in the very beginning Bobby James Galaxy had been content to work this latest con and milk it for all its worth, he found in the last day or so that the dreams that were speaking to him had gone beyond his own selfishness and seemed to speak to him with a real need. Where in the beginning it had been easy to whip a bunch of half-witted Lurkers up into a frenzy with tales of how rotten the aliens were (after all, aliens had more money than they had, had more of everything than they had, which made envy an easy sin to conjure), now, suddenly, it had become something else.

Suddenly, Bobby James Galaxy . . . *believed* what he was selling.

It was odd as hell, but there it was. Where in his first revival meeting yesterday he had pushed all the buttons, said all the right things to get the yokels to shell out, now he was going back to them with *real* fire in his eyes, a real taste for blood in his belly. Holding up that gun (a leftover from his smuggling days) as he had, had been merely another con job. But now, Bobby James Galaxy really *did* want to kill Minbari and Centauri and Narn (oh, my).

After all, con was just the first part of conviction, wasn't it?

And if the Lord had hand-picked Bobby James Galaxy to do his bidding of wiping every alien entity from the dirty face of the universe—well, who was Bobby to argue?

In his quarters, stripped to his Skivvies, covered in sweat, Bobby James Galaxy kneeled on his floor and prayed—prayed as he never had before. He held his hands together so fervently that he thought they might meld into one.

"Lord," he prayed, "give me guidance, show me the path to take, the road to travel."

Hearing nothing, Bobby James Galaxy picked up the fine leather belt he had so recently bought with many credits on the black market (the Drazi, who were such fine hucksters themselves, might be the first to go).

Lifting his eyes to heaven, Bobby James Galaxy again pleaded with the Lord for guidance, gripping the belt in one hand and then snapping it over his head until the buckle hit his own back, cutting deep.

Blood flowed, and still Bobby James Galaxy prayed.

"Lord, please tell me what you want!"

The belt snapped; blood flowed.

For the first time in his life, Harold Schneckelheimer wept tears not for himself, but for all mankind, for all his brothers in the human race.

"Lord, please show me something! Let me see what you will use this poor vessel that is my body for!"

Finally, in the throes of pain, Bobby James Galaxy was given a sign.

"Yes, Lord! Yes!"

Instantly, he dropped the bloody belt and curled into a fetal ball on his cold floor.

Bobby James Galaxy closed his eyes.

And slept.

And dreamed, as the Lord had told him to dream, not of cons but of conviction, and of Minbari heads on poles, and Centauri entrails on the ground, and of Drazi dead scattered like grains of salt of the barren plain of Babylon 5, which burned from end to end with holy and righteous fire.

CHAPTER 32

TAKING the last of his sleeping pills, Dr. Stephen Franklin nevertheless dreamed.

It was the worst nightmare he had ever had. Even as he sank into slumber he tried to analyze why it was so vivid this time: was it because the Worm was so close? Because the accumulation of pills was having a rebound effect, neutralizing their effect and making the dreams worse? He would have to study that when he woke up . . .

But then, after forty hours of straight work, punctuated only by one short, pill-assisted rest period, he dropped down into dreaming sleep:

And was in his Medlab, on his back, strapped to a gurney.

Only there was nothing wrong with him. He knew that; felt it.

And he was surrounded by . . . aliens.

Only now all of his curiosity was gone. Only repulsion and fear remained. Which was horrible in itself, because he had spent so many years studying alien physiognomy and medicine, with something approaching love. And now, to feel like this . . .

There was a reason, though. For here he was surrounded in the darkened Medlab by all the alien patients he had ever treated. There was a single light shining on him, and in the outer shadows he saw them move around him, circling, with medical instruments in their hands.

And now, he knew, they were going to study *him* . . .

Dr. Franklin awoke from his dream covered in sweat. He had called out, and now one of his technicians was at the door, looking in on him.

"Doctor, are you all right?"

Franklin sat up on his cot, took a few breaths, and said, "No, I'm not. I have to see Captain Sheridan right away."

"I'll tell him you're coming."

"Thank you. How many survivors were there from that Bay 8 collision?"

"Two. Both from the shuttle."

"No one survived the *Pegasus*?"

"No, Doctor."

Franklin took a deep breath. "I'll be up in a minute." He'd forced himself off the stims and onto the sedative/opiate only after an embarrassing error in Medlab. And now he felt even shakier than he'd been before his sleep.

The technician let the door close behind her.

Still trembling, feeling the sweat dry on his skin now, Stephen Franklin took a few more breaths before rising shakily from the cot to check on one thing before going to see the captain.

In the briefing room, Captain Sheridan said, "I'll call off their use immediately." The captain looked even worse than the last time Franklin had seen him. There were dark circles under his eyes, and a piece of his hair was sticking straight up. But then, Franklin had looked in a mirror and hadn't liked what he'd seen there, either.

"I think it's best," Dr. Franklin said. "I was going to recommend that all security forces be given one, but after what I just experienced that could be a disaster. I did a quick experiment before coming over here, and what I experienced has nothing to do with the pills themselves. It has to be the proximity of the Worm."

"That's just great. So now we've lost our one weapon against it. Is there a chance you could come up with anything else?"

Franklin shook his head. "I've been trying, but everything is basically a derivative of the first pills."

"All right," the captain said. "Thanks for trying. I know this is a silly question, but how are things in Medlab?"

"Our beds are full. I've taken over two adjacent

rooms, as well as the Alpha Wing ready room. I'll be putting patients in closets next."

"I'm sorry I can't give you more help. But I have nothing in reserve. There is no traffic coming into Babylon 5. The Epsilon jump gate has been shut down, and Earthforce refused to send any troops before that happened. I was told there were none near the sector, and none to spare. I think they were afraid that if fresh Earthforce troops came in, it would scare the Minbari. Sheridan looked pensive.

"Captain," Dr. Franklin said tactfully, "how . . . have your own dreams been?"

"I've just been thinking about that, Doctor. They're not good ones. And they involve Ambassador Delenn."

"Do you feel . . . as if you might act them out? In other words, bring them beyond the dreams themselves?"

With tired eyes, Sheridan looked at the physician.

"I hope not, Doctor," he said.

"I . . . don't want to overly alarm you, but it occurs to me that what happened to me in my most recent dream, in terms of the vividness and reality of it, might be a precursor to what will happen on B5. In other words, as the Worm gets closer, the dreams will become so vivid that we will not be able to distinguish them from reality."

"In other words, we will act out our dreams."

"Precisely."

"Doctor," the captain said, "I have the distinct and horrible feeling that that is why Earth Central has been isolating itself from us. If this station goes down, they want to have as little to do with it as possible."

Franklin nodded.

"We can't let that happen, Doctor. No matter what, we can't let Babylon 5 be destroyed from within. I don't know how much it will help at this point, but I'm declaring a state of emergency on board the station. We've got to do everything we can to get this under control."

At that moment, Dr. Franklin wished more than anything else in the world that he had a pill to give Captain Sheridan that could ease the look of anguish and borderline despair that was on his face. Babylon 5 was a dream itself—a good dream—and it would be a horrible irony if bad dreams—nightmares—destroyed it.

"Then we'll just have to do everything we can to see that that doesn't happen, Captain."

Sheridan nodded. "Yes we will, Doctor."

CHAPTER 33

GARIBALDI entered Command and Control with what almost looked like a smile on his face.

"Well, I've made no progress on finding Londo," he reported to Sheridan and Ivanova, "but at least I've got something to show for my day's work."

He motioned to a security officer at the door, who left, returning a moment later with Dr. Creighton Laramie in handcuffs. The doctor's scowl was all the evidence needed that he was not pleased.

"I give you," Garibaldi said with a flair, "our spy."

"Is this true, Doctor?" Captain Sheridan asked.

Laramie only scowled.

Garibaldi said, "Oh, it's true, all right. I checked up on his company, Barker Industries. Turns out they're involved in all kinds of black-box operations. I also traced his transmitter, down on Brown deck. I followed him to it. He had it hidden in a storage locker."

"Doctor, do you have anything to say?"

"Only that you'll have plenty to answer for to Earth Central. My mission was completely valid—"

"And illegal," Captain Sheridan said. "You were sending illicit transmissions from my station and that puts you in big trouble no matter who you're working for."

Laramie's scowl deepened.

"See if you can find room in the brig for him, Chief," the captain ordered.

"Yes, sir. It will be my pleasure, even though the cells are mighty crowded at the moment. Perhaps accommodations with a bunch of Lurkers would suit you, Doctor? I have a few who haven't bathed in a while . . ."

Still proud of himself, Garibaldi led Laramie out.

"That's one problem solved," the captain said.

"Out of a thousand," Commander Ivanova replied. "We've had another accident, though this one minor, in Bay 6. Three other bays are completely out of our control, taken over by armed thugs. At least they have some sort of training in docking procedures, and so far no one has been killed."

"Can't we get them back under our control?"

"Not without a full-scale assault. And with what? There are brushfire wars all over B5. Some of Garibaldi's men haven't slept since this mess began. The ones that have are almost useless when they wake up. Five of them are under restraints now; after taking a nap they woke up and beat a Centauri senseless."

"What we needed was Earthforce help," Captain Sheridan said.

"And they won't give it to us."

Captain Sheridan turned to the curved windows, which were filled now with the sight of the Worm.

"It won't be long," he said, "before we know just what that thing has in store for us."

Lennier awoke.

How long had it been? He didn't know. Days? Hours?

He winced when he moved his hand. It hurt. He brought it up to his eyes and saw that his entire hand was covered in a dressing; it was especially thick around his wrist.

What had happened?

He didn't remember.

He sat up, noticing that his quarters were unusually dark. He brightened them, and stared for a moment at the blank spot on the far wall where something had been . . .

A mirror?

Yes, that was it.

Suddenly, anger filled him.

Yes, he remembered now: the insult from the woman in the hallway, when the human had bumped into him and walked on without apologizing.

That was not something that could be taken lightly.

Not at all.

Lennier had been foolish enough to take out his anger on the mirror, instead of on the woman herself.

Lennier remembered the dreams now; suddenly, they did not seem like nightmares at all.

They seemed like guidance.

Now, Lennier knew exactly what to do.

Thirty minutes later, dressed in a loincloth and bearing a metal pole topped with a sliver of metal he had fashioned himself into a spear, Lennier boldly walked the corridors outside his quarters searching for the woman who had jostled him.

What had she looked like? Did it matter? She was a human, and that was enough. The first human to come along would do.

Rounding a corner, the Minbari was faced with a harried-looking female technician bearing a tray of electronic parts.

Lennier went into a crouch, brought the dull end of the spear up under the tray, and knocked it from the startled technician's grasp.

"Hey, what are you—" the technician began to say.

"Defend yourself, Earth scum!" Lennier cried, twirling the spear in his grip so that the sharpened point came up into view. Tentatively, he jabbed it at the technician, driving her back.

"You're crazy!" the tech said, turning to flee.

Lennier ran a few steps after her, then stopped to watch her run.

"Ha ha!" he shouted, brandishing the weapon in front of him. "No one crosses this Minbari's path, lest he die!"

Hiking up his loincloth, pleased with himself, Lennier marched on, looking for more technicians to fight.

CHAPTER 34

"CAPTAIN, I think you should see this."

For a moment, Sheridan didn't recognize Commander Ivanova's voice on his link; he realized that he had been staring off into space, trying not to nod off at his office desk, and that his link had probably sounded more than once.

"What is it, Commander?" he said, mustering strength.

"We've scanned a squadron of Earthforce fighters just entering our sector through the Epsilon jump gate. They're heading straight for the Worm."

"I can't believe I'm hearing this," Sheridan said.

"Believe it, sir. I've tried to raise them but get no response."

"Keep trying. I'll be there in a few minutes, after I call Earth Central."

Immediately, Sheridan rose, walked to the command office's communication screen, and opened the gold channel.

Hilton Dowd, the unpleasant official from president Morgan Clark's office, looked as if he had been waiting for the call.

"Can I help you, Captain Sheridan?"

Controlling his anger, the captain said, "I want to know why Earthforce fighters are on their way to the Worm."

The man's lips tightened in a suppressed smile. "Why, they're going to attack it, of course."

"That's madness! You have no idea what will happen if you show hostility toward the Worm!"

"Relax, Captain. After all, we're doing it to protect Babylon 5 . . ."

"Have you notified the Minbari of this? For that matter, what about the other members of the Advisory Council?"

"That's . . . not something we had time to do."

"Are you trying to start a war?"

Now Dowd's smile vanished. "Exactly the opposite, Captain. We're trying to prevent one. If we show that we're unafraid of the Worm, then our . . . allies, and others, will see that we are unafraid of any eventuality."

"You have to call them off immediately!"

"That's impossible, Captain."

Sheridan knew that the man was about to sign

off; his attention had begun to wander, but suddenly it came back to Captain Sheridan.

"Oh, by the way, Captain Sheridan. There is a man on Babylon 5 by the name of Creighton Laramie. He is to be treated with the utmost respect, and be given any equipment or help he might desire."

"I know about Creighton Laramie. At the moment he's in our brig."

"What!"

"He's a spy. He was caught making unauthorized transmissions from B5."

Sheridan could almost study the workings of the man's mind by studying his face; he was obviously turning over options and trying not to get angry.

"You are authorized to let him go immediately."

"As soon as we've finished our investigation into his activities."

"He must—"

Sheridan cut the transmission off.

"Oops," he said, knowing that what he had done would only buy him a little time as far as Laramie went.

The Observation Dome was a beehive of activity.

"Report," Sheridan said, when he arrived, taking over the command console.

Commander Ivanova said, "A squadron of Starfury fighters is heading at top speed for the Worm. Scan technicians tell me their weapons systems are activated."

Sheridan frowned. "Have you been able to raise them?"

"They're not listening to us. At least they're not answering."

"All right, Commander," Sheridan said to Ivanova. "You handle things here. Perhaps those Starfuries will talk to us if we talk to them up close and personal."

"Sir—" Ivanova began, realizing what Sheridan had in mind.

The captain held up a hand for silence. "Carry on," he said, leaving the dome.

In the Alpha Wing ready room, Captain Sheridan, looking almost eager, said, "It'll actually keep me awake to get my hands on a Starfury again."

"Actually," Alpha Wing pilot Lauren Simmons said, "it'll be nice just to get out of this madhouse for a while."

Around them, the ready room, which had been converted into an overflow medical area, was filled with makeshift beds and moaning patients. Medical technicians, half dead on their feet, walked through the maze of equipment and cots.

In a few minutes they had made their way through this jumble to the Cobra bay, into their suits and command helmets, and were each climbing into an F23 Starfury.

Sheridan heard Ivanova in his helmet going through a priority drop checklist; as the last item was ticked off the Commander said, "Ready to drop, sir?"

Sheridan looked over at Simmons, who gave him a thumbs-up sign.

"Ready," the captain said.

"Then prepare to launch," Ivanova said. "On my mark." A few seconds went by, then the commander said "Drop!"

The two Starfuries dropped out of Cobra bay into space, instantly curving up away from B5 due to the station's spin. Instantly Sheridan and Simmons hit their thrusters.

"Good luck, Captain!" Ivanova called.

The Starfuries leveled off at full thrusters toward the Worm.

"Give us an ETA on the Worm," Sheridan said, "in comparison with the Earthforce fighters."

"Give me a second, sir." After a moment Ivanova came back on line. "You'll get there barely five minutes before they do."

"Very good. We'll be back as soon as we can."

"Yes, sir."

There was silence in Sheridan's helmet for a few moments, and then Simmons asked, "Captain?"

"Yes, Simmons."

"Um . . . What exactly are we doing out here?"

"You'll see. Just do what I do."

Simmons mumbled, "I hate when anyone tells me that . . ."

Just as Ivanova had predicted, they reached the Worm before the Earthforce squadron. Out across the vast rolling green plain of the Worm, they could see the other fighters bearing down on them in precise formation.

"Now remember, Simmons," Captain Sheridan

said into the Alpha Wing pilot's helmet, "do everything I do."

"Yes, sir."

"Good. I'm now going to full readiness on all my weapon systems."

Simmons gulped. "Yes, sir."

"Now I'm lining myself up to target the lead ship in the Earthforce squadron."

Simmons said nothing.

"You doing what I say, Simmons?" Sheridan asked.

"Done, sir."

"Got him targeted in your sights?"

"Uh, yes."

"Good. Now just wait, and let me do the talking."

"That would be my pleasure, sir."

Sheridan opened an outside channel to the Earthforce squadron.

"Attention, approaching Starfuries. This is Captain John Sheridan, Commander of Babylon 5. I have your lead fighter in my sights, and will fire on it if I have to, as will Lauren Simmons of Alpha Wing, who is manning the Starfury beside me. You may defend yourselves if you want to, but I want you to realize two things. First, your command ship *will* be destroyed if hostilities commence and its pilot killed; and, secondly, you will have opened fire on a fellow officer and the commander of the only surviving Babylon station. I can promise you that, whatever the outcome of our little dogfight, there will be grave consequences for your actions.

"I don't care what orders you were given by Earth Central: I am giving you orders in the field now, as your commanding officer. You will abort your attack on the Worm immediately. What is your response?"

There was silence as the squadron of Earthforce fighters continued to bear down on them.

To Simmons, Sheridan said, "Are your weapons fully armed?"

"Yes, sir."

"Fire on my command."

The Earthforce squadron continued toward them at full thrusters, and Sheridan made sure the lead fighter was dead in his sights.

Sheridan said into his command helmet, leaving the channel open for the Earthforce squad to hear: "Ready, Simmons?"

"Ready."

"Aim."

"Right!"

"Fi—"

"Wait, sir! Captain Sheridan, sir!" came an urgent call from the Earthforce squad. The lead Starfury veered off, as the others scattered behind him.

"I'm listening," Sheridan said calmly.

"Permission requested to abort current mission, sir."

"Permission granted. You have my assurance that I take full responsibility for your actions."

"Yes, sir."

"Fall in behind us," Sheridan said, disarming his weapon systems and banking his Starfury around to point back toward B5. "And follow us back."

"Yes, sir."

Before Sheridan could finish his turn, there came a bright flash in the vicinity of the Worm.

"I don't believe it!" Simmons said.

The captain looked back to see a huge Centauri battle cruiser emerging from hyperspace near the Worm. There was a final flash as its self-generated jump point collapsed, leaving the ship looming outside the Worm.

Immediately, it began to fire into the green band, peppering it up and down with weapon surges which shot right through the Worm.

As if angry, the cruiser moved ever closer, firing again and again.

"Commander Ivanova!" Captain Sheridan called into his helmet.

"Yes, Captain, I see it!"

"Get in touch with the Centauri government immediately!"

"I've already tried."

"What about the battle cruiser?"

"They won't answer either, sir!"

Changing frequencies, Sheridan tried to raise the battle cruiser himself.

"Centauri cruiser! This is Captain John Sheridan, commander of Babylon 5!"

But then there came another barrage of fire, from the opposite direction—and suddenly Sheridan and the others, as well as the Worm, were caught in the middle of a battle between the Centauri transport and a newly arrived covey of renegade Narn fighters.

CHAPTER 35

THERE were three battle-scarred Narn fighters, and despite the insanity of the situation, Sheridan was almost relieved to hear G'Kar's voice in his helmet.

"Captain, I must apologize for our unfortunate confluence under these circumstances."

"G'Kar, where did you get those fighters?" Sheridan asked.

"They are . . . Narn underground ships, Captain, saved for a case of criminal aggression such as this. They were . . . hidden in the shadow of the planet. If you will kindly remove yourself from the area, we will obliterate the Centauri cruiser." Underlying G'Kar's polite tone was a hint of rabid hatred.

Mustering a measure of calm, Sheridan said, "I

would be much more beholden to you, G'Kar, if you would kindly turn around and go back to B5."

"I'm afraid that's impossible, Captain. Narn honor is at stake. The very presence of the Centauri in the universe is an abomination against G'Quan. They must be exterminated, now. Please move aside. I would hate for you to get in the middle of this."

"I already am in the middle of it!"

In his helmet, the Centauri ship came on line.

"If you truly are Captain John Sheridan," came an insulting voice, "I would appreciate it if you would move your ships so that I might annihilate the Narn dogs hiding behind your skirts."

"Good-bye, Captain," G'Kar said.

Instantly, the three Narn vessels went to full thrusters and headed around Sheridan's Starfury toward the Centauri battle cruiser.

Space was filled with traded shots, and Sheridan helplessly listened to radio traffic.

"I think we've hit their vortex generator!" came an excited Narn voice.

"Prepare to die, Narn dogs!" a Centauri voice spat.

A Centauri shot hit one of G'Kar's flanking ships head-on and it disintegrated into pieces. At the same time, the two remaining Narn fighters, ignoring Sheridan's pleas, bore down directly on the transport.

The Earthforce squadron leader's voice came into the captain's helmet.

"Want us to get into this, sir?"

"No," Sheridan ordered. "Stay out of it."

As they watched, one of the Narn ships hit the battle cruiser dead center, while the other seemed to be swallowed whole by it.

"Cap—" came G'Kar's voice, before it was cut off.

"Lord, do you think . . ." Simmons blurted out.

"I don't know what happened to him. But I think we should get back to Babylon 5 before things get worse."

Leading all the Starfuries, Sheridan turned away from the recently completed battle, leaving the Centauri ship, seemingly crippled, to rake new fire upon the Worm.

CHAPTER 36

AFTER getting the Starfuries docked in Cobra bay, Captain Sheridan made his way back to the Observation Dome.

To Ivanova he said, "I want a formal complaint issued to the Centauri government," he said.

"Already done," Ivanova said.

The captain studied his command console.

"What about the effects of the Centauri firing on the Worm?"

"All scans show no effect at all."

"It didn't flinch?"

"Not one nonexistent particle showed any change whatsoever."

"In other words," Sheridan said wryly, "it still doesn't exist."

"Something like that," Ivanova countered. She seemed disturbed by something.

"What is it now?" the captain demanded. "Drazi swinging from the chandeliers? Mass conversion to the Consortium of Live Eaters?"

Commander Ivanova winced.

"I'm waiting for your bad news, Commander."

Ivanova faced him. "While you were gone . . . we had to let Creighton Laramie go."

"Let him go! By whose authorization?"

"President Clark himself. He would have chewed you out had you been here. So he chewed me out instead. And gave Laramie an instant pardon for anything he's done—even gum chewing was included, I think."

Some of the captain's anger dissipated.

"I'm sorry you had to go through that, Commander. Did Clark give any reason at all?"

"None. But I got the feeling . . ."

"Yes, Commander?"

"I got the feeling that they want very much for Laramie to keep studying this thing. He's holed up in his lab now, studying the effects of the Centauri attack on the Worm."

"In other words, he was sent here as a spy, but more importantly, he was sent here to study the Worm. Whatever black-box things they can glean from it, they want before anyone else can get their hands on it."

Ivanova nodded.

"In other words," Sheridan continued, "it's just

the same old game of seeing if they can turn the Worm into a weapon."

Commander Ivanova said, "It looks that way to me, too."

"Well, all right then," Captain Sheridan said. "We'll let him do his work. But we'll monitor everything he does."

"You mean . . ."

Sheridan nodded. "Get me Garibaldi."

The security chief had just nodded off and was heading into his rotten nightmare about crashing on the alien planet when his link went off.

He listened for a few moments, then said, "Right away."

Twenty minutes later, as Dr. Creighton Laramie was lured away from his lab by an "urgent" message from Commander Ivanova, Garibaldi set to work thoroughly bugging the room.

In less than ten minutes he was finished and had his kit repacked.

He passed Laramie on the way out.

"Can I help you?" the doctor said in an unfriendly tone.

"Uh, yeah, as a matter of fact you can," Garibaldi said. He opened his kit and took out a small screwdriver. He held it out toward Laramie.

"Can you use this? I have an extra and thought you might need it."

With a snort, Laramie brushed past Garibaldi and entered his lab, ordering the door to shut behind him.

* * *

Garibaldi returned to Command and Control and handed Captain Sheridan a data crystal.

"Here's everything Laramie knows so far—which isn't much. He's got some scanning equipment in that lab of his I've never even seen, but most of it turned up zilch. There was one interesting tidbit on there, though."

"And that was?" Sheridan asked.

"Apparently Laramie was scanning very vigorously while the Centauri battle cruiser was shooting at the Worm. There were notations next to the reading that said, 'almost there.' "

"Almost there—what do you make of it?"

"It could mean he's almost found something."

Sheridan nodded. "Or it could mean that something was 'almost there.' "

Garibaldi nodded. "Remember what Laramie said while we were out scanning the Worm in the shuttle? About the Worm being a ghost of something?"

Thoughtfully, Sheridan said, "And if you remember, Martina Coles mentioned the word ghost, too."

"And she implied that Kosh sensed the same thing," Garibaldi added.

The captain said, "You know, Chief, ever since this began I've gotten the feeling that we were just getting a taste of what the Worm is. I think that's what Laramie means."

"Yeah," Garibaldi said, "but what does he mean by it?"

CHAPTER 37

ON Captain Sheridan's communications screen, the Centauri battle cruiser commander spoke with contempt. "You are Captain John Sheridan, I presume?"

"That's right," Sheridan said.

"You may listen to my demands—"

Sheridan held up a hand. "Hold it right there. You won't be giving me any demands."

On the screen, the Centauri began to bluster with anger, then thought better of it. "Very well. Perhaps if you merely *listen,* you will be able to understand the drift of my meaning."

Sheridan ignored the insult.

"What is it you want?" the captain asked.

"We have . . . certain repairs to undertake. I

would appreciate it if you would allow us close proximity with Babylon 5 until those repairs can be completed, in ten hours or so."

Of course they wanted to stay close, since they wouldn't be able to jump out of the region before the Worm arrived in only six hours. "I can do better than that. I'm prepared to offer you full docking privileges and the use of our facilities, if you will help me with a certain diplomatic problem."

"You speak of course of the Narn, G'Kar?"

"Yes," Sheridan said, hope springing up in him that G'Kar was alive after all.

The Centauri gave a cynical smile. "We will discuss G'Kar in a moment. And no thank you, but I think we will pass on your offer of direct assistance. For one thing, I hear things on Babylon 5 are rather . . . chaotic at the moment, and I would not want that chaos to infect my crew. For another thing, I think it would be better for . . . military reasons if we stay undocked from Babylon 5."

"I don't understand," Sheridan said.

"Proximity will be fine, Captain Sheridan. And now to direct matters: I understand our ambassador, Londo Mollari, is being unlawfully held on board Babylon 5?"

"He has been kidnapped, yes. We are doing everything we can to find him."

"Apparently that is not much. So I have another solution to this criminal problem."

The Centauri made a curt motion to someone offscreen, and a figure was now thrust into view. It was G'Kar, bruised but not humbled.

"Captain," he said in simple greeting to Sheridan.

The Narn was pulled away, and the Centauri ship's commander resumed his place on screen.

"Our decree is a simple one to understand. You may broadcast it throughout Babylon 5 if you wish. I'm sure it will have the desired effect. In short, if Ambassador Mollari is not released by the criminal Narn who have taken him, our captive will be executed."

"You can't do that!" Sheridan protested.

"Believe me, Captain, I will."

"If you kill him, Ambassador Mollari will surely be killed."

"G'Kar is a criminal and a dog! His Narn cohorts may watch his execution on-screen in exactly six hours. That is a nice round number—the same time at which the green Worm will reach Babylon 5. And please, Captain, do not attempt to interfere with military force. For we will resist with every means at our disposal."

The screen went blank, and then flashed on again with the Centauri's smug face.

"Oh, and thank you for letting us have proximity privileges with B5, Captain."

Again, the screen went out, and stayed that way.

Immediately, Captain Sheridan consulted with Ivanova and Garibaldi.

"They'll execute him, all right," Garibaldi declared.

"The only reason they haven't taken G'Kar away

with them," Ivanova said, "is that the Narns were able to partially destroy their vortex generator."

"And the Epsilon jump gate was shut down again after that Starfury squadron was let through, so they can't get away that way," Sheridan added.

Garibaldi said, "Right. So what do we do about G'Kar?"

Sheridan pondered, then asked, "Would it help if we broadcast the Centauri threat to execute G'Kar throughout Babylon 5? Do you think the Narn would let Londo go?"

Garibaldi frowned. "It could go either way. Anything could happen. But then again, everything *is* happening already, so . . . why not?"

"Let's try it," Sheridan said. "I'll broadcast a message with it. Maybe it will lead to negotiations."

Twenty minutes later Sheridan appeared on every communications screen still working on Babylon 5, explaining the situation and vowing to work as a go-between if negotiations were to start.

"These are trying times on Babylon 5, and I hope that this can be the beginning of a new era, where we put aside our differences and work together. The Worm has affected us all. I'm afraid we are coming close to living up to our ancient Earth namesake, the city of Babylon. I would hate to see Babylon 5 become a place where no one speaks the language of understanding and restraint."

* * *

Twenty minutes after that and Sheridan had his answer: a message was received from the Narns holding Ambassador Mollari stating with finality that he, too, would be executed at exactly the time that the Worm passed over Babylon 5.

CHAPTER 38

THE Worm drew closer.

Implacable, inscrutable, unknowable—the green mysterious ribbon which existed and didn't exist made its inexorable way toward Babylon 5. It was now less than five hours away.

And the nightmares began to become reality.

In her quarters, Martina Coles lay in a fetal position, eyes tightly closed, sobbing, trying to ignore the sound in her head and the memories in her mind.

In an equipment locker whose door had been forced open, the Minbari Lennier laughed as he fashioned weapon after weapon, using whatever materials were at hand; by his feet were a veritable pile of spears, each with a tip sharper and more deadly than the last.

Delenn, the Minbari ambassador, after heroically driving herself without further sleep as long as possible, locked herself within her quarters and fell into a morass of nightmares in which she battled, and was slain by, Captain John Sheridan over and over.

Captain Sheridan, nodding off briefly at the desk in his command office, once more saw his face in vivid horror transformed into that of a Minbari.

Michael Garibaldi, between fielding frantic calls in Security Central, tried to piece together the puzzle of the Worm and come up with a reason for its effect on B5 and a way to combat its effects.

On every deck, in every corner of Babylon 5, new fights were breaking out. Three-quarters of the cargo bays were now out of the control of B5 security forces; in Bay 4, a security team had fought its way onto a cargo transport, driving off everyone but the pilot at gunpoint. They'd taken their leave of Babylon 5.

Centauri now fought Narn on sight, and even within the same species or race, the smallest difference of opinion could lead to blows or bloodshed.

* * *

In Medlab, Dr. Stephen Franklin was overwhelmed; patients lay in corridors, and medical supplies were running low.

And on the cold floor of his room, the Reverend Bobby James Galaxy woke up from his dream of epiphany, which had not been a nightmare to him at all but a revelation, and suddenly he knew not only what God wanted, but how to bring about God's will—and destroy Babylon 5.

CHAPTER 39

"I literally thought things couldn't get any worse." Commander Ivanova looked haunted. The bags under her eyes attested to her lack of sleep; her hands trembled with it. Outside the Observation Dome's windows, the Worm loomed like an oppressive cloud, only an hour away.

And now the worst possible thing of all was happening.

"Can he do it? Can he really blow up Babylon 5?" Captain Sheridan asked in disbelief. Waking from his brief nightmare he had made his way groggily to Command and Control only to find that a madman was now threatening B5 with destruction.

"He can do it, if he's done what he says he's done," Ivanova answered.

On the communications screen, the beaming face of Bobby James Galaxy said, "Do I have the pleasure of addressing Captain Sheridan?"

"You do," Sheridan said grimly. "And I know who you are. What I don't know is why in hell you're threatening my station."

Bobby James Galaxy beamed. "Captain! I threaten nothing! I'm speaking of salvation!"

"And you feel it's up to you to kill nearly a quarter of a million people to save them?"

"Yes! The Lord awaits! Salvation awaits! For today is Judgment Day, Captain!"

"And what if I don't agree with you?"

"But you must! That is what the entity you call the Worm tells us! For the Worm is God, and when he passes over us, we must throw ourselves into His hands!"

"And that's why you've reconfigured the power grid on Brown Deck so that it will back into the rest of the system and blow us to bits as the Worm passes over?"

"Yes! Flinging us all right into His arms!"

"And what if that Worm isn't God?"

"Captain, do not doubt my message. Please, join me in thanks!"

Bobby James Galaxy fell to his knees and began to pray. Somewhere offscreen came the voices of tens, possibly hundreds, of other voices, singing the praises of God.

Bobby James shouted, "For the Lord is good!"

"Amen!" came the chorus in answer.

"And the Lord is just!"

"Amen! Amen!"

"And within the hour, we will be in His hands!"

"Amen!"

Sheridan said, in disgust, "Off," and the screen went off.

Garibaldi entered, looking wounded and exhausted.

"Any luck, Garibaldi?" Sheridan inquired, though the security chief's face already gave away the answer.

"Nothing. I couldn't get close. This Galaxy nut already had won over more than half the Lurkers before he got this idea into his head—and then he won over Fermi's Angels, and that was that."

"Did you talk to the Angels? Didn't you say you had some influence with them?"

"I talked with them, but all they would do between prayers was ask me to join them. This just fits into every one of their core beliefs. And they'll be proving themselves right and the Life in Transition group wrong."

"Along with the rest of us."

Garibaldi nodded. "And believe me, they knew what they were doing with the power grid on Brown deck. Those guys are better at physics than they are at motorcycles."

"Did you threaten them?"

Garibaldi laughed humorlessly. "With what? They've already won over thirty of my officers. All I could threaten them with was not letting them see pictures of the Ninja ZX-11 cycle I built with Lennier."

Trying to humor herself, Ivanova said, "Did that win them over?"

"Almost. They still want to see the cycle—and then blow up B5."

In frustration, Captain Sheridan said, "What can we do to stop them?"

Garibaldi said, "Not much, at the moment. They're heavily armed, and have the whole Brown deck sealed off but good. The only thing we could do is try to hold off or isolate that backup power surge they've got planned."

"How do we do that?"

There was silence for a moment, and then Garibaldi looked at Ivanova and Sheridan.

"Dr. Creighton Laramie?" he asked.

Laramie would not open the door to his lab.

"Emergency override," Garibaldi said out loud. "Open door."

Still the door wouldn't open.

"Damn," the security chief muttered. Then he shouted, "Laramie? I'll blow a hole in the door if I have to!"

From the other side came Laramie's unhappy voice: "Why should I let you in? I know how heavily you bugged this room—isn't that enough?"

"Not even close. Without your help, Doctor, Babylon 5 will cease to exist in less than one hour."

After a moment Laramie ordered the door to open, and stood before Garibaldi, a small PPG pistol in his hand.

"There's no reason for me to trust you," Laramie

said. The effects of little or no sleep, and of Laramie's own undoubted nightmares, showed on his features.

"And none for me to trust you," Garibaldi answered. "But do we have a choice?"

After a long moment Laramie tucked the gun into his belt, and said, "Come in."

After hearing Garibaldi give the details of what the Fermi's Angels had done, Laramie said, "There's a chance I can stop them from the main power grid. If I send another surge to meet theirs head-on, in phase, the two will neutralize one another."

"What effect would it have on B5?"

"A momentary loss of power. Like a brownout."

"Can you do it?"

"Yes. But it will take me thirty minutes to set it up. And I want my equipment here to continue to run while I'm gone, and your assurance that you'll remove your bugs later."

Garibaldi said, "That's not a problem," and then hailed Ivanova on his link.

"Commander, how long do we have until the Worm passes over Babylon 5?"

Ivanova's strained voice said, "Thirty-five minutes."

Garibaldi looked at Dr. Creighton Laramie evenly. "I'd better get you where you need to go."

CHAPTER 40

AFTER setting Creighton Laramie up, and with only twenty minutes until the Worm passed over Babylon 5, Garibaldi found himself alone in a hallway faced with a very belligerent Lennier.

The Minbari, dressed in nothing but a loincloth, held himself in a crouch with a homemade spear at the ready in front of him.

"Lennier? Is that really you?" Garibaldi asked.

"Of course it is!" Lennier laughed.

Garibaldi took a deep breath and said, half to himself, "I just don't have time for this . . ."

"For what?" Lennier shouted. "For dying?"

The Minbari rushed forward, jabbing at Garibaldi with his spear.

"Hey! Watch that!" the security chief said, moving aside to avoid the thrust. All levity gone now, he said, "Lennier, what's wrong with you?"

"Nothing!" Lennier announced. "Something merely wonderful has happened to me!"

Garibaldi realized that the Minbari Martina had warned him about must be Lennier. "Lennier—this is me! Mike Garibaldi! Don't you know me? Don't you remember the motorcycle we built together?"

"That was the past, Garibaldi—this is now!" Lennier made a feint with the weapon. "I've been doing much thinking about the Worm, and discovered that what it's done is merely strip away the artifice that we dress ourselves in! When there's nothing left but core beliefs, what do you have? You have fear, and hatred, of the other!" Again he feinted with the spear. "And you, Garibaldi, are the other!"

Garibaldi, tired of playing games, started to pull out his pistol to disable the Minbari—but, with a quick move Garibaldi didn't think the youth capable of, Lennier leapt forward, jabbing his weapon deeply into the security chief's side.

"Hey!" Garibaldi cried out, before dropping his weapon; he tried to take a breath and instead collapsed to the ground, groaning as he rolled slowly onto his back.

He looked up to see Lennier standing over him, wild-eyed, the spear held tightly in his hand—

And then blackness descended.

"Where's the chief!" Captain Sheridan demanded.

"I can't raise him!" Ivanova said. She took a quick glance out the Observation Dome's windows at the Worm; the cosmos might as well have been green, the way the Worm dominated the now-starless sky. "The last I heard from him he was on his way back from setting up Dr. Laramie."

"Did he give Laramie a link?"

"Yes."

Captain Sheridan spoke into his own link: "Sheridan to Laramie. Doctor, can you hear me?"

Laramie's voice, sounding preoccupied, said, "Yes, Captain?"

"How's it coming?"

"I should just make it, if I'm left alone."

The link went out; then chimed again almost immediately.

"Sheridan here."

"Captain? This is Delenn. I must see you immediately."

"Delenn? Where are you?"

She sounded very disturbed. "In the Zen Gardens. I'll meet you by the shuttle station. Please come."

Captain Sheridan said to Ivanova, "Commander, you're in charge here. If you hear anything from Garibaldi or Laramie, call me immediately."

He looked at the Worm.

"How long?" he asked.

Ivanova knew the answer without checking. "Twenty minutes."

* * *

In fifteen minutes, Sheridan was stepping off the shuttle platform in the Zen Gardens.

It was a scene of madness. What was designed as a place of peace and refuge, of greenery and open space, had become just another battleground on B5.

Two Centauri, bearing long sticks, ran by after a pair of bruised Narn. The flash of phased plasma generator weapons split the normally still air. Nearby, in a fountain, two other figures, usually friendly members of the League of Non-Aligned Worlds, wrestled, each trying to drown the other in the shallow water.

"Captain—thank you for coming."

Sheridan turned to see Delenn rushing at him with what looked like an ax in her hands; she took a crude swing and the side of the blade caught the captain on the shoulder, sending him down to one knee.

"Delenn—what are you doing!"

"This was my nightmare, Captain—only in my nightmare it was you who killed me. Now I will make sure that if one of us is to die, it will be you."

She moved past him into a stand of bushes; a moment later she reemerged, bearing a smaller ax, which she tossed on the ground and kicked toward Sheridan.

"It would not be noble of me to refuse you a weapon, Captain."

As Sheridan picked the ax up, feeling a surge of self-preservation and an odd, surpressed hatred, Delenn rushed at him again. He held his own weapon up and blocked her blow, and suddenly the battle was joined in earnest as he drove her back and took his own first swing at her.

"If it's battle you want, Ambassador—I'll give it to you!"

Delenn moved back, breathing hard now; and then Sheridan rushed forward, ax held high in one hand.

Sheridan's link sounded.

"Captain!" came Ivanova's desperate voice.

"I can't talk to you now!" Sheridan snapped, and charged forward at Delenn.

The Minbari held her own ax up to ward off the blow, throwing the captain's momentum to one side. Again his link chimed as he stumbled and fell to the ground, Delenn locked in a grip with him now.

"Captain Sheridan!" came Commander Ivanova's voice. "I have two communication screen transmissions—one from the Narn holding Londo and the other from the Centauri ship holding G'Kar. Both ambassadors are on screen. Their captors say they will execute them in two minutes, when the Worm passes over!"

Sheridan ignored the link's message; his eyes locked with Delenn's, mirroring her hatred—for a split second he saw the image of his nightmare: himself as Minbari, hating anything that was not Minbari.

"No!" Sheridan shouted. The Minbari were the enemy. He pushed Delenn away and scrambled to his feet. A hatred like he'd never known welled up in him and he rushed at the ambassador, striking blow after blow which she countered until she was driven to her knees, holding her weapon up before her.

"Is this how I am to die?" Delenn said, all strength suddenly leaving her as she dropped her ax and looked up in horror at the captain.

"Yes!" Sheridan cried, raising his weapon high over his head in fury—

And then the lights in Babylon 5 went out.

CHAPTER 41

THE Worm passed through Babylon 5.

Dr. Creighton Laramie, working furiously to counter the power surge his instruments told him had been unleashed down on Brown deck, felt the Worm pass through. He had no scanners for that—but he felt, at the moment the Worm went through him, *something.*

Something that was there—and then instantly gone.

Every being on Babylon 5 felt it; every passenger on every ship in the vicinity of the station felt it; all those on the Centauri battle cruiser holding G'Kar ready for execution felt it. As the Worm reached the inactive Epsilon jump gate, the refugees who had fled the station in the lines of cruisers and transports and stolen shuttles felt the Worm pass through them—and disappear.

On Babylon 5, on every deck, in every corner, every living entity felt the Worm pass through. The Reverend Bobby James Galaxy felt it, even as his hand gave the signal for the Fermi's Angels to send the power surge that would destroy the station. He felt something—and then nothing.

And then the lights went out, as Dr. Laramie's own power surge met Bobby James Galaxy's, throwing Babylon 5 into temporary darkness even as the Worm passed through—and disappeared.

As power was restored at Command and Control, Commander Ivanova desperately studied the twin communications screens which had gone blank for a moment.

On them, to her relief, were still views of two very alive ambassadors.

"Babylon 5 control," came a voice from the Narns holding Londo Mollari, "we are willing to negotiate the Centauri ambassador's release.

Instantly, Ivanova contacted the Centauri ship.

"The Narns are willing to let Ambassador Mollari go if you let G'Kar go free—do you agree?"

"We will . . . think about this proposition," came the reply; and then, a scant minute later, the Centauri ship's commander himself came on-line and said, curtly, "We agree to the exchange. We will effect it as soon as possible."

"Thank you," Ivanova said, and instantly signed

off both communication screens and said into her link, "Dr. Laramie, are you there?"

"Yes, Commander, I hear you," Laramie said drolly.

"Is Babylon 5 in any further danger from power surges?"

"I should think not. I've calibrated the main grid to counter any further surges sent from Brown deck. I myself am heading back to my laboratory. I have some interesting data to study, I'm sure."

"Thank you, Doctor."

Characteristically, Laramie merely signed off without saying anything further.

When Ivanova again tried to contact Garibaldi, there was no answer from the chief.

But, after a moment, his link was activated.

"Um, Commander Ivanova?" came a scared-sounding voice.

"Yes, this is Ivanova. Who is this?"

"Lennier."

Puzzled, Ivanova said, "Lennier? Is Chief Garibaldi there?"

"Yes, he is, Commander," Lennier said; the young Minbari's voice was a monotone.

"Can you put him on?"

"No, I can't Commander. I suggest you send help immediately. The chief . . . needs medical attention."

"What happened to him?" Ivanova asked.

"I . . . think I've killed him."

CHAPTER 42

CAPTAIN John Sheridan and Minbari Ambassador Delenn felt the Worm pass through.

As power was restored in the Zen Gardens, and the lights came back on, they found themselves facing one another, holding weapons.

As if the ax had scorched her, Ambassador Delenn dropped it to the ground. Captain Sheridan let his own weapon fall and stared down at it as if it were a foreign thing.

"Ambassador, I don't know what to say," Sheridan said, his voice filled with embarrassment.

Mortified, unable to look at Sheridan, Delenn said, "It was I, Captain, who lured you down here. It was I who had the bad dreams that led to this."

"I had my own bad dreams," Sheridan said, daring to look at Delenn. He feared he might see an enemy, but instead he saw a friend. He added, in a low voice, "If you wish, nothing will be said of this."

"I could not wish for more, Captain." Her eyes met his. "And I am so sorry."

Sheridan turned his hands palm upward and studied them as if they were not his own. "I . . . could have *killed* you," he said in disbelief.

"This was a horrible episode, worse than any nightmare," Delenn agreed.

Feeling obligated, Sheridan took a step forward.

Delenn went stiff. "Please, Captain, no. I must . . . think on these things."

Abruptly, she turned and fled, leaving Sheridan to once more study his hands in wonder.

After a while, regaining his composure, the captain made his way through a suddenly quiet Zen Gardens toward the shuttle back to the Observation Dome. On the way, he saw stunned residents of Babylon 5 looking as if they were waking from a dream. In the fountain, the two former opponents from the League of Non-Aligned Worlds now stood staring at one another like strangers. Weapons, both homemade and professionally fashioned, had been dropped in place, abandoned. Overhead, the mag-lev shuttle rode slowly toward its station, as if nothing had happened.

But much—too much—had happened.

CHAPTER 43

MICHAEL Garibaldi awoke on Dr. Franklin's operating table and was relieved to see Franklin smiling.

"Feeling better?" the doctor asked.

"Fit as a fiddle—am I dead?" Garibaldi joked.

"No, but Lennier thought you were. He's in deep depression over it, too. There's a lot of that going around on B5 at the moment. But to tell you the truth, it's been a hell of a lot easier dealing with that than dealing with what I had before."

"How long have I been out?"

"About three hours. You had a collapsed lung."

"Ouch. No wonder I couldn't breathe right. When will you let me out of here?"

"If you're a good boy, you can leave in another

ten hours. You'll have to take it easy for a while, though."

"Won't that be a relief."

"To all of us," Franklin said.

Garibaldi tried to laugh, and winced at the pain.

At Command and Control, things had returned to a form of normalcy.

Tired but smiling, Commander Ivanova reported to Captain Sheridan: "Both Londo and G'Kar have been released. Which doesn't mean the Centauri and Narns suddenly love one another—but it's a start."

Sheridan nodded. "I've already had three communications from Londo complaining about the conditions he had to endure at the hands of his kidnappers. He wants nothing less than all their heads mounted on poles."

"Which brings up a point," Ivanova said, seriously. "Namely, what about punishment? Even though the Worm is gone, we've still got a mess on our hands. Dr. Franklin says the almost murderous rage that the Worm was causing has lessened, but that there are still a lot of residual hostilities. In other words, they may not be trying to kill each other in the halls anymore, but they're still shouting at one another."

"I know," Sheridan concurred. "I've already fielded more complaints about the Life in Transition group, and the Trinocular Film Festival bunch is demanding that we rig up a new theater so that they can continue showing their films. They say they won't pay a credit on their contract costs unless we accommodate them immediately."

"At least the Reverend Bobby James Galaxy is in custody," Ivanova said.

"You can credit that to Garibaldi's men coming to their senses," Captain Sheridan responded. "I'm sure the chief will have plenty of disciplinary business to take care of with his officers, but at least they're all on our side again. Speaking of which, how is Garibaldi?"

"He's resting and will be able to come to your meeting at oh eight hundred hours."

"Good. I want all of us to get some rest before that meeting. And the others?"

"In his charming way, Dr. Laramie said he would be there, and Martina Coles said she would attend, also."

"And Kosh?"

"He was reluctant—but he'll be there."

"Good. I want as much input as possible. It will be hard enough as it is to write a report on the Worm to satisfy Earth Central, and the more I know about it the better."

Sheridan turned to stare out through the Observation Dome's curved windows, where nothing but black space and stars ruled again. "Have you . . . thought about what you felt when the Worm went through us?" he asked.

Ivanova paused before answering. "Yes, I've thought about it. It was like . . . nothing else I've ever felt. But I don't know how to describe it."

"Neither do I," Sheridan said, turning to look at

her. "But I know in my gut that it was *something.* It wasn't nothing, no matter what the readings say."

"The closest I can describe it is to say it was like . . . something very high up looked down at me for a tiny moment, and then moved on."

Sheridan nodded slowly. "Something like that . . ."

"What do you think happened to it? Where did it go?"

"I don't know . . ." Sheridan said thoughtfully. "Back where it came from, I guess. The scans certainly showed nothing after it passed through Babylon 5. One tech who watched it visually said it went out, like turning off a switch."

"I wonder if we'll ever know exactly what it was," Ivanova said.

"I doubt it," the captain said, turning back to the Dome's windows to look out at space again. "Somehow I doubt it . . ."

CHAPTER 44

In her quarters, Martina Coles was getting used to being herself again.

The buzzing in her head was gone. And the *something,* whatever it had been, was gone also.

And, oddly, she felt as if she almost knew what it was.

Shaking her head, she continued to pack, knowing that as soon as things returned to normal on Babylon 5 she would be leaving, on her way to her new job. The Epsilon jump gate had been reopened, and as soon as her ship arrived she would be on it and gone from this place.

Another odd thing: she felt almost sad leaving it.

Her door chime sounded.

"Come in," she said.

The door slid open, revealing a wan and bandaged but grinning Michael Garibaldi.

"Hello," Garibaldi said, walking gingerly into the room.

Martina managed a slight smile and said, "Hello."

Garibaldi said, "I just wanted to make sure you were all right."

"I'm fine . . . now," Martina said. She started to turn back to her packing but instead faced Garibaldi and looked him straight in the eye.

"I want to thank you for helping me," she said.

"It was nothing. All I did was give you a horse pill and make you drink some water."

"It was more than that. It was kindness. You got close to me. It's very hard for me to let anyone get close. It used to be hard for me to thank anyone for anything."

Garibaldi waved a hand in dismissal. "Don't be so hard on yourself, Martina—"

"I'm not being hard. I'm being objective. Some . . . things happened to me a long time ago which made me what I am. I am very much an antisocial person. I have a reluctance to get along with others. However, this recent episode with the Worm has showed me things about myself. Some conflict with others is healthy. But too much is as bad as none at all. It makes one stagnant. It is not healthy." Her face softened into a real smile, and suddenly she stepped forward and kissed Garibaldi on the cheek. "Thank you again."

Garibaldi found himself blushing. "Uh . . . you're welcome," he said.

Embarrassed, Martina had turned back to her packing.

"Uh, I'll see you later at Captain Sheridan's meeting?" Garibaldi asked.

"Yes," Martina said.

"See you then," Garibaldi said, turning and walking from the room.

When the door had closed, Martina looked up at it and smiled and said, softly, "Yes."

On his way to Security Central Garibaldi stopped at Lennier's quarters, but the Minbari was not in. Turning away from the closed door, Garibaldi almost ran into Lennier, who was hurrying, eyes downcast, back to his quarters.

With a gasp Lennier staggered back; instantly, his eyes were downcast again.

"Hey, Lennier, how's it going?" Garibaldi asked jovially.

The young Minbari began to tremble. "I may not talk with you, sir . . ." he said.

"Hey, what is this? Don't you like me anymore?"

"I have . . . done you the greatest dishonor. I have done a terrible thing that can never be righted."

Keeping his voice light, Garibaldi said, "What did you do? Cheat at poker?"

Briefly, Lennier raised his eyes to look at Garibaldi. "You know what I speak of, sir."

Garibaldi pointed to his bandaged side. "What, this? It's nothing—just a scrape!"

"I tried to kill you," Lennier whispered.

"But you didn't succeed! You're lousy with spears!" Garibaldi let his voice get serious, and put his hand out to rest on the young Minbari's shoulder; momentarily, Lennier flinched, and then let the hand stay. "Lennier," he said, "it wasn't *you* who tried to kill me. It was a little part of you that's in all of us, a little part way down at our core that we never let out. It's where our deepest fears and feelings are, the place we retreat to when there's absolutely nowhere else to go. It's the place that makes us afraid of anything that's different from ourselves."

Though Lennier would still not look at him, Garibaldi knew the young Minbari was listening intently.

"I've been thinking about this a lot, Lennier," Garibaldi continued. "I think what happened with the Worm was that it somehow unleashed all these fears and core feelings in the form of nightmares. Eventually, the nightmares got so intense that they got out of control and became real." He tightened his grip on Lennier's shoulder. "But that's not us, Lennier—that's not who we are. It's just a tiny part of us, put there for self-defense. It's not anything you can change or wish away, either. It's something we tame and live with."

Lennier was looking at him now, and Garibaldi took his hand from the Minbari's shoulder and gave him a light punch instead.

"Hey," the chief said, laughing, "you think I'd build a motorcycle with a guy who wanted to kill me? Which reminds me, I got some great new ideas from the Fermi's Angels, and I think we can improve on the ZX-11. Unfortunately for us, most of the Angels are in the brig at the moment, but I think I can impound one of their cycles to study. That is, if you're willing . . . ?"

Lennier gave a slight smile. "It would be my privilege," he said. "And you know, I have been thinking about what has happened myself, and it has given me some possible insight. What if growth and evolution within a particular race of beings, and between different races of beings, is dependent on the continual conflict between different systems of belief?"

"We've certainly had enough of that lately," Garibaldi said wryly.

"Look at the history of countless worlds," Lennier continued. "Where are the races of 'saints,' beings who have brought their species to the point of perfection? Perhaps paradise is another name for stagnation and death."

"So you're saying it's healthy for all this fighting and bickering to take place?"

"To a point."

"You know, you may have something there—"

The security chief's link chimed.

"Garibaldi here," he said into it.

"Uh, Chief," came the voice of one of his ensigns, "we can use you over in the Main Hall. There's another demonstration, so far peaceful, against the LITs. And Templeton says they could also use you over at the Zocolo; there's been some looting. And also—"

"I'll be right there," Garibaldi said, cutting the ensign off. To Lennier, who was now smiling, he said, "I've got to go. Things are still crazy around here. Some of those fears and core feelings I talked about haven't been tamed yet. But I think you've just given me a way to get things back to normal . . ."

CHAPTER 45

CAPTAIN John Sheridan, looking fit and rested after six hours of peaceful sleep, called the meeting in the briefing room to order.

"I've invited you all here so that we can try to understand as much as we can about the nature of the Worm," he said. "It's very important that our report be as open and complete as possible; the final version will be distributed in its entirety on data crystal to anyone wishing to study it—and our findings in capsule form will be published in every newspaper on Babylon 5 and be available to any other media which request it.

"You've all heard Security Chief Garibaldi's report regarding his thoughts on the nature of the nightmares—I trust you all found it as interesting as

I did. Dr. Franklin, do you have anything to add to what Chief Garibaldi says?"

Franklin shook his head. "It's probably as good an explanation as any. None of the scans I was able to do turned up anything concrete—but as a theory, Chief Garibaldi's is about as good as we're going to get. Though," he added smiling, "I'm sure that once the academics and conspiracy buffs get a hold of our report, they'll come up with new—if bizarre—theories of their own."

Sheridan smiled. "All right, then. I think perhaps it's time to hear from Dr. Creighton Laramie. Doctor?"

Laramie took a sip from the water glass in front of him, nodded tersely, and said, "You'll remember, Captain Sheridan, that I mentioned to you that my scanning instruments had picked up the shadow of something that wasn't really there. I would have to say that was an apt description. What I got on my instruments when the Worm passed through Babylon 5 was only a shadow, a whisper, of something that wasn't really there.

"We got a glimpse of something, of a somewhere else. It was here, and yet it wasn't. That doesn't make scientific sense, but I think it's as close as we're going to come. The 'somewhere else' I'm talking about isn't hyperspace; there isn't any jump gate to the place the presence belongs. It's another plane, somewhere else."

Laramie took another sip of water and set the glass carefully down. He held his hands out.

"Think about walking along in the woods on

Earth. You come to a stream, put one foot in the water as you cross and then you walk on, leaving the stream behind. You don't belong in that water world, but for an instant you were there. If you were preoccupied at the time, thinking about something else, you hardly noticed where you were. But anything living in that stream knew of your presence. You raised holy hell down there."

Laramie put his hands down flat on the table and said, "The Worm was the man walking in the woods—and we were the stream."

"Dr. Laramie," Captain Sheridan said, "were you able to find out anything concrete about this . . . other place?"

"Nothing I'm willing to discuss," Laramie said stonily. He turned to regard Garibaldi. "And if you remember our agreement, Chief, you were to remove all your bugging equipment from my lab."

Garibaldi said, "I kept my word. Everything that was mine was removed." Garibaldi looked at Sheridan and gave a small wink.

"Then whatever findings I have will remain my property, and the property of my company, Barker Industries," Laramie said. "If you wish to discuss this matter, please bring it up with Earth Central."

Captain Sheridan said, "There's no need for antagonism, Doctor. We're all very grateful for your actions in saving Babylon 5."

Laramie rose. "Then I'd appreciate it if you'd leave me alone, until I'm able to finish my work and depart Babylon 5. Which will be as soon as possible."

"Of course—" Sheridan began, but Laramie, without another word, strode from the room.

"Still as charismatic as ever," Garibaldi said.

Captain Sheridan, recovering, turned to Martina Coles and said, "Would you share your impressions with us?"

Martina said, "I can only say that the Worm did represent . . . something. I don't know what. It was something that may not, as Dr. Laramie stated, have been aware of us. I do think that Ambassador Kosh may be better suited to answer your question . . ."

All eyes turned to Kosh, who stood in a corner of the room, immersed in his inscrutable environment suit.

"Ambassador Kosh, do you have anything to share with us?"

After a long moment, the communications section of the ambassador's suit irised open and a musical tinkling emerged with the word: "No."

Startled, Captain Sheridan said, diplomatically, "I realize your reluctance to be here, but I don't quite understand it. In your audience with Ms. Coles you made her aware that there was, indeed, another presence out there in the spot where we saw the Worm. She described it as a shadow, as did Dr. Laramie. She also said that you seemed to be shocked by its existence. Isn't there anything you can tell us about its origin? Anything you can share with us?"

"I can . . . share nothing."

Abruptly, Kosh turned and left the room.

"Well . . ." Captain Sheridan said, "under the circumstances, that will end our meeting." He said to Garibaldi, "Chief, I'd like to see you for a moment."

Garibaldi nodded. "Right."

As Martina Coles filed past him, she took Garibaldi's hand. "Until next time," she said.

Garibaldi, feeling not at all foolish, raised her delicate hand to his lips and kissed it.

"Until next time," he said.

Martina smiled and said, "And thank you again."

When the room had emptied, Garibaldi and Sheridan sat down across from one another.

"First off," Garibaldi said, "I've got data crystals on everything Laramie recorded in his lab when the Worm passed through B5."

"How . . . ?"

"I promised him I'd remove all my bugs. But I didn't promise him I'd remove yours."

Sheridan laughed. "Do the data show anything?"

"Laramie's got a surprise coming, because they don't show much more than what he already knows. So his big ideas about making new weapons out of this are just so much smoke."

"Thank God for that, anyway."

"Second bit of business," Garibaldi said. "Did you get the feeling that Kosh was upset?"

"Very upset," Sheridan said. "Whatever happened when the Worm went through here, it affected him deeply. I only wish he would tell us what he knows."

"I can find out what a guy like Laramie knows, but not somebody like Kosh. I do get the feeling that if there were any further danger to B5, he'd let us know."

"Yes . . ." the captain said. "Outside of that, we just have to respect his privacy."

"And third," Garibaldi continued, "I have a plan on how to finally get Babylon 5 back into order. But I'll need you to trust me."

"What's the plan?"

"Well, in theory, it's simple. There's no way to bring all these factions still fighting it out together. We'll never get them to agree on anything. And if we let them go on the way they are they'll tear what's left of B5 to pieces. So here's what I have in mind . . ."

When Garibaldi had finished, Captain Sheridan said, "Do you really think it will work?"

"Outside of calling in massive amounts of Earth-force personnel, and getting Earth Central's sticky fingers involved in our affairs, I think it's the only way."

"And if it works, we retain our autonomy," Sheridan said. "For that reason alone, I'm willing to give you a shot."

"And there's one other reason I'd like to do this," Garibaldi said, standing up gingerly to favor his still sore right side.

"What's that?" the captain asked.

Garibaldi grinned. "It could be a hell of a lot of fun."

Outside the briefing room, Ambassador Delenn was waiting for Captain Sheridan.

"Captain," she said, haltingly.

Sheridan, as embarrassed as the Minbari Ambassador, said, "It's . . . good to see you, Ambassador."

After a moment, Delenn said, "And it is good to see you, Captain." The beginnings of a smile formed on her lips, and she glanced at the floor. "I only wanted to say that I hope that what has . . . happened between us will not affect our . . . relationship adversely."

Sheridan said, "We were not ourselves, Ambassador."

Delenn brought her eyes up and looked at the captain evenly. After a long moment she said, in a resolute voice, "I have thought long and hard about this, Captain, and you are right: we were not ourselves."

"But I hope we can be ourselves again," Sheridan said.

Delenn, smiling, said, "Yes, Captain, I hope we can."

CHAPTER 46

"ARE you sure about this?" Commander Ivanova, marching beside Chief Garibaldi, said uncertainly.

"Trust me," Garibaldi said.

Behind them marched forty handpicked security officers, armed to the teeth. But Garibaldi knew he would have no use for the weapons. The only weapon he needed was his mouth.

They started at what was left of the conference room where the Life in Transition group had reestablished themselves.

"These guys just don't give up," Ivanova said in wonder, viewing the wreckage of the room, as well as the huddled group of hard-core LIT members who, though black and blue and half stripped of their elaborate, nonorganic clothing, still chanted their beliefs, surrounded by an angry mob of dissenters, among them a few Fermi's Angels, including Silicon, who had not participated in Reverend Bobby James Galaxy's antics.

"You are mistakes," the LITs chanted. "You are unnatural. You are random."

"And you Lite-heads are dog meat!" Silicon shouted. Her taunt met with a chorus of hoots and affirmative sounds.

Seemingly oblivious, the LITs continued to chant: "You are mistakes. You are unnatural. You are ra—"

"That's *it!*" Garibaldi shouted, marching straight through the crowd with his troops forming a wedge behind him. Dissenters were thrown every which way.

The security chief stopped before the LITs.

"Who's in charge of your group?" he demanded.

After a momentary silence, the LITs began to chant again.

"You are mistakes. You are—"

Garibaldi grabbed the nearest LIT and shook him.

"I said who's in charge?"

The LIT pointed meekly to a particular LIT, whose clothing had larger sections of mica attached to it.

Garibaldi grabbed the leader's arm and said, "You're coming with me."

"Atta boy, Chief!" Silicon cheered.

"And you, too," Garibaldi said, reaching out to

take Silicon by the arm. He passed the two leaders back to his troops, who secured them in custody.

Silicon pouted, "Aw, Chief! And I woulda given you another chance to ride with me!"

"Onward!" Garibaldi ordered.

It took hours for them to sweep through the different sections of Babylon 5, picking up leaders as they went. The amount of destruction and debris was disheartening, but Garibaldi never faltered in his quest to gather the leaders of every squabbling faction on board B5, including G'Kar and Londo Mollari.

"This is *outrageous*!" Londo protested as he was escorted from his quarters. "Your government will hear of this!"

"Relax, Londo," Garibaldi said. "We're doing it to everybody. And don't get any ideas about getting in touch with that Centauri battle cruiser—it fixed its vortex generator and left four hours ago."

"Still! This is an outrage that will not be tolerated!"

Smiling, Garibaldi passed him back to his troops, where he was secured with the others.

Finally the sweep was finished, and Garibaldi had all his captives herded into a conference room which had been cleaned up and outfitted with a huge round table and chairs. At the door the security chief, smiling pleasantly, greeted them as they were ushered in.

"Find a seat, please, and sit down. And listen up!"

Nearly fifty pair (except for the representative of the Trinocular Film Festival) of eyes regarded Garibaldi with barely concealed animosity.

"Right now," the security chief began, "you all hate me, and, frankly, I don't care. You don't have to get along with me. What you do have to do is figure out how to get along with each other.

"The Worm—whatever it was—is gone. It's over. I don't give a damn what you people are for or against. We're done with this, you understand? There will be a tribunal. You will elect a chairperson and a committee from among your factions. It is *your* tribunal that will decide who is responsible, and in what proportion, for the damage that has occurred on Babylon 5. When that is completed, you *will* pay for those damages. The selection of this tribunal will begin here and now. All aggressive behavior will cease. Those of you who are prone to threaten Babylon 5 with legal and or diplomatic action"—here he turned a hard glance on Londo—"may do so if you wish, but those threats will be made from somewhere *off* of this station."

A roar of anger rose from the crowd as he finished.

"Any hostile action or argument will be met with immediate ejection from Babylon 5, regardless of your status or condition. Remember, B5 is still under a state of emergency. I can do this."

Garibaldi turned and left the conference room as

the roar rose even higher, and motioned for his security guards to close and lock it behind him.

"And make sure nobody leaves until they do what they're supposed to," he said.

Ivanova, waiting for him in the hall, shook her head in wonder. "You said, 'That's all,' and left? That's *not* all, Garibaldi. They'll have your hide *and* your pension, if they can."

Garibaldi grinned. "Sure they will. If they ever get around to it. They'll be fighting over this impossible tribunal I tossed in their laps for quite a while."

Ivanova smiled. "I wonder how long it will take them to form a committee from their factions—much less name a chairperson?"

"Oh . . . somewhere in the next millennium is my best guess. Somewhere around the time it takes to figure out what the Worm was."

Ivanova's demeanor darkened. "A lot of terrible things have happened on Babylon 5 the last few days. Do you think we'll ever get back to normal?"

"What's normal?" Garibaldi commented. "We'll do our best, and keep moving ahead, like we always do." He nodded back toward the noisy conference room. "At least we'll have that bunch out of our hair for a while."

Ivanova sighed, and then she said, "Oh, I forgot to tell you: while you were in there giving your speech, Captain Sheridan informed me that an old buddy of yours was about to leave B5. He asked the captain to give you a message."

"What was it?" Garibaldi asked.

"He said his name was Bill Smollens, and that his ship was in ever lousier shape than when you saw it last. Seems it got beat up pretty bad in some of the rioting. He wants you to take another ride through the Epsilon jump gate with him."

"Ha! Fat chance!" Garibaldi laughed. "I'd rather lock myself back there in that conference room than get on Smollens's junk heap again! I'll tell him I'm home, and mean to stay here for a while!"

Commander Ivanova laughed.

They walked on, Garibaldi beginning to whistle as the riotous sounds from the conference room faded behind him.

CHAPTER 47

In his methane-shrouded quarters in the Alien Sector, Kosh, the Vorlon ambassador, once again replayed the passing of the Worm in the recesses of his alien mind.

It was a moment he could never forget, and which would never cease to affect him. As methane fog swirled around him, he once more felt it just as he had felt it then.

As the Worm had passed through, he felt sensed-touched and almost knew the presence as it vanished. In that brief moment of *almost,* he had reached out with his thoughts, seeking to grasp hold.

What are you . . . ? he had asked.

And, as the Worm vanished, pulled away back into that other place, had come the reply, like the briefest of whispers tendriling against his mind: *What are* you?